MW01140485

Modern Day Bride

Moment in Time, Volume 3

Lexy Timms

Published by Dark Shadow Publishing, 2016.

MODERN DAY BRIDE

First edition. November 22, 2016.

Written by Lexy Timms.

Also by Lexy Timms

Alpha Bad Boy Motorcycle Club Triology
Alpha Biker

Conquering Warrior Series
Ruthless

Diamond in the Rough Anthology
Billionaire Rock
Billionaire Rock - part 2

Dominating PA Series
Her Personal Assistant - Part 1
Her Personal Assistant - Part 2
Her Personal Assistant - Part 3
Her Personal Assistant Box Set

Firehouse Romance Series
Caught in Flames
Burning With Desire
Craving the Heat
Firehouse Romance Complete Collection

Fortune Riders MC Series
Billionaire Biker
Billionaire Ransom
Billionaire Misery

Hades' Spawn Motorcycle Club
One You Can't Forget
One That Got Away

One That Came Back
One You Never Leave
Hades' Spawn MC Complete Series

Heart of the Battle Series
Celtic Viking
Celtic Rune
Celtic Mann
Heart of the Battle Series Box Set

Justice Series
Seeking Justice
Finding Justice
Chasing Justice
Pursuing Justice
Justice - Complete Series

Love You Series
Love Life: Billionaire Dance School Hot Romance
Need Love
My Love

Managing the Bosses Series
The Boss
The Boss Too
Who's the Boss Now
Love the Boss
I Do the Boss
Wife to the Boss
Employed by the Boss
Brother to the Boss
Senior Advisor to the Boss
Forever the Boss
Gift for the Boss - Novella 3.5

Moment in Time
Highlander's Bride
Victorian Bride
Modern Day Bride
A Royal Bride
Forever the Bride

R&S Rich and Single Series
Alex Reid
Parker

Saving Forever
Saving Forever - Part 1
Saving Forever - Part 2
Saving Forever - Part 3
Saving Forever - Part 4
Saving Forever - Part 5
Saving Forever - Part 6
Saving Forever Part 7
Saving Forever - Part 8

Southern Romance Series
Little Love Affair
Siege of the Heart
Freedom Forever
Soldier's Fortune

Tattooist Series
Confession of a Tattooist
Surrender of a Tattooist
Heart of a Tattooist

Tennessee Romance
Whisky Lullaby

Whisky Melody
Whisky Harmony

The Debt
The Debt: Part 1 - Damn Horse
The Debt: Complete Collection

The University of Gatica Series
The Recruiting Trip
Faster
Higher
Stronger
Dominate
No Rush

Undercover Series
Perfect For Me
Perfect For You
Perfect For Us

Unknown Identity Series
Unknown
Unexposed
Unpublished

Standalone
Wash
Loving Charity
Summer Lovin'
Christmas Magic: A Romance Anthology
Love & College
Billionaire Heart
First Love
Frisky and Fun Romance Box Collection

Managing the Bosses Box Set #1-3

Modern Day Bride

Moment in Time: Book #3
By Lexy Timms

A Moment in Time Series

Find Lexy Timms:

Lexy Timms Newsletter:
http://eepurl.com/9i0vD
Lexy Timms Facebook Page:
https://www.facebook.com/SavingForever

Lexy Timms Website:
http://lexytimms.wix.com/savingforever

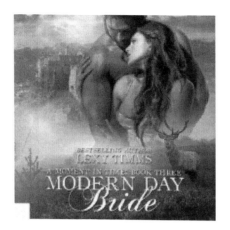

Description

You were made to be with me, as I was made to love you. No moment in time can take that away from us.

The sounds of a storm wakes Mya in the middle of the night. Except instead of a storm, a war is raging outside the window. She had no idea what time it is, or even the date. She doesn't know how she ended up in the building, or who the handsome soldier that saves her is.

She feels connected to him, and his older worldly ways. A stranger and yet she knows things about him—intimate things, like the scar on his chest, the way his hair curls around her fingers when she runs her hand through it.

Pieces of a puzzle they don't understand, begin to fit together. Destiny seems to be pushing them together, but why? Just when they are on the verge of figuring out their connection, the devastating war tears them apart again.

You were given this life because you're strong enough to live it.

Prologue

Kayden ran, but he knew he wasn't moving fast enough.

He wasn't going to make it in time.

Springing forward with all the momentum he could throw into his stride, he leapt. Time seemed to stand still. For an instant, he hung suspended over the fallen tree that had blocked his path. Around him, the bare branches were hands reaching out in the darkness and slow him down. The tall grass had frozen mid-motion, caught in a graceful curve.

Then he connected again with the earth. Time jarred into motion once more, and he was pressing onward. His lungs cried out for air as his heart beat furiously against the bones protecting it, and he panted for every breath.

Overhead, a jagged bolt of lightning sliced through the dark sky, its electric veins breaking and stretching to light his path and illuminating the fields around him with an eerie yellow-white light. He ignored the rumbling thunder that followed, and the burn of muscle that begged him to stop, or at least slow down.

He leapt again, catching a glimpse of what he was after. Hope seared through him and pushed himself harder. Faster. Another bolt sliced through the sky. In its glow, he saw her stumble. Urgency pressed at his core. He had to hurry. He had to save her. If he could just reach her. He was so close.

A scorching pain ripped through his body.

It was pain without source, without reason. There was no wound opening in his skin. There was only the pain, dizzyingly strong. Kayden's eyes lost focus on the path ahead, and the world became a blur of green. He staggered.

Kayden tried to regain his balance, but his head still spun with pain. He stumbled, and hit the grass rolling. Still trying to recover, he tried to heave himself up. Back to his feet. He had to get back to her.

But it was too late. It wouldn't matter what he did any longer. He had already failed.

Far away, Kayden woke with a start. His breath came out in gasps as he sat up on a bed, his body covered in sweat. He grabbed the bottle beside him on the dresser, gulping down the dregs of the burning liquor inside. It did nothing to erase the images printed across the backs of his eyelids, imprinted in his mind.

The dream had happened again.

Chapter 1

The constant rumbling of thunder brought her back to consciousness. It had started off in the distance, its grumbles in the sky echoing and moving closer, and as they grew near she felt the roll of them up through the earth, rattling her bones. She pressed her eyes tighter shut as lightning flashed against the backs of her eyelids. The storm seemed to be circling around her. Coming in close, then moving out and circling back around again.

It would be on top of her soon.

She waited for the inevitable rainfall to begin.

As another burst of light shattered the night – the thundering crash following instantaneously, without so much as a second between sight and sound, Mya shifted where she lay, rolling onto her stomach to hide her face against the earth.

Except she wasn't lying on grass as she had thought. The surface she lay on was hard, chill against her skin. The edges of a dream played on her mind.

She'd been sleeping, she realized. Dreaming. Her mind had made the mountains in the distance, the rolling hills and lush grass seem like a memory, clear as yesterday. Mya moved her arms to hide the zigzagging light from her eyes. She wanted to go back to the dream.

There had been a forest on her right, rushing water to her left, and soft, fresh grass under her feet. It had felt glorious. Her heart had been pumping hard as she ran. She'd never felt so free. Her mate, her lover, raced beside her toward the edge of the cliff. She'd wanted to see the view, smell the bitter salt scent of the waves, hear the sounds of the sea. Her handsome, strong partner had no problem keeping up with her. He ran effortlessly beside, muscle rippling under his skin and his dark eyes fixed ahead on their goal.

Another crash of thunder roared above her, shaking the house where she lay. Pellets of rain battered down on the roof and side of the house. Mya turned, and winced as the side of her head pressed against the hard ground below her. Eyes still closed, she fought against the nausea that welled in her stomach from the sharp pain.

She wasn't on a bed, she realized. Maybe she'd fallen off as she dreamed, the storm throwing her senses off kilter.

Gingerly running her fingertips along her scalp, she found a hard bump, followed by tender pain. She wondered what she'd hit it against. A table? What else would be beside her?

Oddly, she couldn't remember. It felt impossible to think clearly over the noise of the storm.

She shivered against the cool floor, and came to a sudden realization.

Damn it. I'm naked.

Finally giving in to the fact that there would be no more sleeping till she moved, she opened her eyes to the darkness around her. As she waited for her eyes to adjust, she felt for a sheet to wrap around her cold body.

Her hand brushed against an overturned chair and she wondered if that was what she'd hit her head on. The thought brought a wave of nausea and instantly a pounding headache. Or maybe the headache had been there all the while and she was just noticing it now.

Struggling slowly, she managed to get up on all fours. Only to lurch to the side as her stomach heaved and she tried to empty its contents. It cramped in protest, and the egg-sulfur smell hanging heavy in the air only brought on another bought of dry-heaving.

The room brightened suddenly as the sky lit with flaming light.

Mya gasped, the nausea and headache momentarily forgotten.

She didn't remember the room.

The place was a mess. As if someone, or many people, had ransacked it. Chairs overturned, tables broken, shards of glass everywhere, a chest of clothes dumped and a closet cupboard's contents mostly emptied. From what she could see, only a single chair stood on its legs, knocked against a wall and tilted to the side, only tenuously hanging on to its upright status.

Amid it all, there was no bed. Not near her or anywhere in the room.

Fraught, she stood and grabbed the piece of clothing closest to her. With shaking hands, she pulled it over her head. She'd assumed it was a shirt but it hung long enough to be a dress. Most likely her dress, she guessed, though she didn't remember ever wearing it before.

She stumbled toward the window, terrified she would step on glass. A pair of lady's shoes hung by their tied shoe-strings over the wooden back of the only piece of furniture still standing upright amidst the rest of the chaos. She pulled them from it and untied the loose knot, wishing another bolt of lightning would brighten the room. The ache in her head came back as she bent down to slip the shoes on.

Straightening, she moved to the window and looked out into the night sky, squinting into the darkness in hopes of finding some recognizable form.

She gasped sharply as she appeared to get her wish and for a long moment the air lit up.

But it was no lightning, and there was no storm.

Instead a battle raged all around her.

The sound of the fighting could just be heard under the boom of the cannons lighting the night sky, pellets and mortar raining down on the building where she stood. She was in the middle of a war.

Watching in horror as the building across from her gave way to whatever had exploded in the side of it, she stepped back, covering her mouth with her hand to stifle the scream rising in her throat.

Who would do this? Why would one clan be so angry with another? What could have possibly happened? The world angry and lost? How had she missed the signs? Or had she missed them at all? Maybe she had known of them, and simply couldn't remember.

The headache pressed against the front of her head, confusing her thoughts.

War.

The dream she'd had was becoming lost in memory. The fresh air, the soft grass, even the freedom she'd felt were all evaporating, warping into this nightmare reality as she watched men in large machines inching along the road below her. A long cannon gun sat at the front of one, and as she stared down at it in confusion the powerful weapon shot at something she could not see.

A tank. The word fluttered in her mind and she grasped it like it might explain what was happening around her, whispered it experimentally.

This wasn't her home, she realized. So where was she?

She hugged the dress closer against her body, more for comfort than to ward against the cold, and, wanting to see where the tank was going, she moved on to the next window, thankful that she had bothered to put the shoes as she found herself sidestepping a set of broken dishes that had been scattered across the floor so that she could reach the sill and watch the road below.

Which side are you on?

Mya had no idea how to answer the question. She just wanted the tank to pass so she could make her way out of the building and somehow find her way home, but that train of thought had her heart suddenly pounding, panic tightening her chest and threatening to cut off her airway. Where was home? Where was she? Who was she?

"Calm down," she told herself, trying to sound firm, but the quiet reassurance rang more than a little hollow, even to her own ears. She tried again. "Calm down, Mya." Mya?

"Mya." Her name was Mya. She knew that much.

What else? She knew home was somewhere with rolling green hills, rising toward the cloud-heavy sky, and salt water nearby. There were lakes and streams there, too.

She replayed her one memory, trying to dredge up further details.

She could run a good distance before tiring, and she was loved. She had a lover somewhere waiting for her. Probably worried sick about her.

No. Wait, she thought, and the calm that she had almost grasped melted away again.

That had been the dream the battle had woken her from. That wasn't memory. The realization confused her further, and another wave of panic threatened, but she refused to give in to it. Focusing on staying back from the window so that she wouldn't be spotted, she craned her neck and stood up on tiptoe, trying to get a better view of the tank, of the road outside. Looking in vain for something, anything, that was familiar. Nothing. *Where am I?*

Behind her she thought she heard a noise, and for a moment she froze. Her heart leapt, beating hard and fast in her chest. She strained to listen over the sound of the chaos outside, over the sound of her heartbeat.

It came again, the creak of a floorboard from just outside the room.

At last! Someone was here to save her!

She spun around, a small smile of relief on her lips. "Thank you..." But the words died on her tongue. Outside another explosion lit the sky, flooding the room with bright light.

A man in uniform she didn't recognize stood in the doorway. His coat seemed strange to her; too big in length, too short in the arms. But it wasn't the coat that caught her attention and stole the words from her lips, or the uniform that he wore. It wasn't the hat that partially covered his features, or even the grim and angry expression on his hard face.

It was the gun he held in his hand. And the fact that it was pointed directly at her.

The barrel clicked as he released the safety.

"What en de hell," he barked the question at her, his accent making the words as hard and unforgiving as his expression, "are you doing 'ere, Fraulein?"

Chapter 2

Mya backed away from the muzzle of the gun, her hands lifted palm up in front of her. Her heart raced, but it felt as though it was somewhere in the vicinity of her throat, making breathing impossible.

"I'm sorry," she whispered, taking another step back, careful not to trip over any of the mess on the floor. "I don't know how I got here. If you can just point me to the closest exit, I'll—"

"Shut up. No one just walks into the middle of a war zone. You're here for a reason, and you're going to tell me what that reason is." He glared at her, his eyes narrowing. "Are you a spy?"

"I honestly don't know why I'm here. I have no idea how I found myself in this place," Mya said, trying to keep her voice steady; she wasn't going to let him hear her beg. However, panic was sending her heart racing. "I had no idea a war was even going on. I've hit my head, and... and I can't remember anything."

The man with the gun stared at her. She couldn't see his face, only the tilt of his head silhouetted against the flickering light from the battle outside. He made a sound that might have been a laugh, if it hadn't been so sharp at the edges. So cold. "I don't think I'm going to believe that story, Fraulein. No one is that unlucky."

She was, apparently, but Mya wasn't sure that pointing that out to the man in front of her would do much good. He didn't seem very inclined to listen.

"Now," he barked, making her jump. "You're going to tell me the truth, and you're going to tell me all of it, or I'll put a bullet through you right here."

"I did tell you the truth!" Mya protested. "I'm not here on purpose. I have no idea where here even is."

"It's a sad day that such a lovely thing has to be put down," the man said, and the growl in his voice sent a cold chill running down Mya's spine.

He was going to kill her, she realized. Right there. Without a second thought. He was going to shoot her, and no one would even know she had died. Were they looking for her, she wondered in the bare moment before the gun would inevitably go off. Did anyone want to bring her home? She supposed she'd never know.

The gun clicked, like the safety was coming off or the man was aiming.

The moment had come. Time was no longer giving her a chance to run.

Mya held her breath and just as she slowly closed her eyes, not wanting the horrible man's face to be the last thing she saw, a movement caught her attention. Her eyes flew open in surprise.

Suddenly there was another man, barreling in through the door. He hit the first from behind, and they went down together in a jumble of limbs, darker shapes against the darkness. Mya swallowed a startled scream. In a flash of light from the doorway beyond, she saw that the second man was darker-haired, and that he wasn't wearing the same uniform as the first. An enemy soldier?

She saw his face, too. Just for an instant in the fickle light. And for a moment she was sure she recognized it. Had she seen him before? Was he here because he knew her? Had he come to her rescue because he was looking for her?

A knife was pulled from somewhere, glinting in the intermittent illumination. Mya watched it rise and then fall, heard it catch against something else with a clang of metal on metal. She couldn't tell who was who any longer, only that they were rolling around on the floor, each of them trying to gain the upper hand. Every time the bombs outside lit up the room, the positions had switched—first one top and then the other, both of them growling and swearing at each other.

He was going to get hurt. The man who had run into the room. Mya took a step forward. She didn't know what she could do to help him, but she had to try. If he was killed it would be her fault. Abruptly it was over much too quickly for her to intervene.

The gun went off with a sharp explosion.

Mya jumped. An instant later, she saw the knife gleaming in a downward arc, and then it was over. One of the men was staggering unsteadily to his feet. The other lay unmoving on the ground. She didn't hear any sound from him. Was he dead? Had a man just died in front of her? Because of her? The thought made her stomach turn over.

But now she had bigger worries. The survivor was turning toward her, and she didn't know who had won. She took a step back, hand pressed over her mouth, and nearly tripped over a box that stood behind her. Her arms pinwheeled for balance, and then the man was there, wrapping his hand around her wrist and catching her before she could tumble backwards. Mya's heart raced.

"Are you hurt?"

Relief ran through her in a rush. His voice wasn't the harsh and guttural voice of the soldier who had pointed the gun at her. It was warmer and softer, the accent at once familiar and oddly comforting. As another blast shook the ground and the light filled the room once more, she could see that the man standing before her with one hand pressed hard to his side was the man who had entered after the first. The one who had undoubtedly saved her life. Mutely, she shook her head by way of answer, not trusting her voice not to shake.

She saw some of the tension go out of him at her answer, but it was back again almost immediately, his eyes sweeping over her like he was trying to determine where she had come from. He dropped her wrist. Mya still felt the lingering heat where his hand had been curled around it.

"What are you doing in here?" he demanded.

Mya stared into dark eyes that filled with the brief flicker of light from beyond the window. She thought she saw there, for an instant, some kind of familiarity. But maybe it had only been a trick of the moment, the same way she had thought when she first saw his face in that brief instant, that she had seen him before. In another room. In another place.

"Do you know me?" she asked, voice quiet. "Do I know you?"

The light flashed, and she saw the expression on his face clearer. It was distant. Concerned. A soldier's expression. Her heart squeezed tight in her chest.

Chapter 3

Mya became aware again, in the relative quiet after the heart-pounding adrenaline of the gun and the fight, that her head ached, pain throbbing through it with each not-so-distant boom. The walls of the little building they stood in shook as the bombs fell. The world spun dizzily around her, and she staggered forward a step, reaching out for something to hold. Her fingers closed around the back of the chair the shoes had been hanging over, but it wobbled in her hand, as unsteady as she was.

There was nothing else but damage in the little room. The other chairs had been knocked over, toppled in the remnants of someone's life. Had it been her own, she wondered again? Or someone else's? And if it was not her home, how had she ended up here, with an aching head and no memory of where she had come from? Her knees buckled. Distantly, she recognized that she was going to fall. The ground rushed up to meet her in the dark.

Except she didn't hit the floor. There were arms around her suddenly, breaking the descent and lowering her gently downward. The soldier who had rescued her once already was holding her, on his knees in the mess, one of his strong arms around her shoulders. Light flashed, and she caught again a glimpse of his face in the gloom—the dark eyes and the high, strong cheekbones, the full mouth and the strong jaw. Dizzy as she was, her heard beat a little faster in her chest. Looking down at her like that, face half-hidden in shadow and then gone entirely as the light faded out once more, he had looked like...

She saw a room, small and dim, filled with firelight in the early evening. The smell of the smoke was heavy on the air, mixing with the cooler scent of the earthen floor and rock walls. The man who had rescued her was there, his hair longer, standing close enough that she could feel the heat of his body against her own. Electric tension sparked between them, the remnants of anger twisting into something else. He had just spoken, she was sure.

Mya looked up at him, and felt words coming out of her mouth, an answer to the ones she couldn't remember.

"Like some sort of what?" she demanded.

"Like some sort of faerie creature," he hissed. "Here to lure me to my doom."

Her hand fisted in his shirt. Her heart was pounding. She glanced down to his lips, remembering the way they had felt on her own, then back, up. The look in his eyes was hot enough to set her aflame. Mya felt like she was burning. She wanted to be closer, wanted their clothes gone, wanted skin on skin contact. She wanted *him*.

"And if I was?" The words were flippant, but they very nearly caught in her throat, her body almost trembling with his nearness and her desire.

He dragged in a ragged breath. "Then I would gladly go."

With the fistful of his shirt she yanked him forward, his body bowing toward hers, and their lips met. It was rough and hungry, hardly leaving space for breath. Big hands curled around her hips and pulled her closer. His tongue ran across her bottom lip and he nipped at it slightly. She gasped and opened her mouth to him and his tongue slipped between her lips, filling her senses with the taste of him. The way his body felt against her own. The room around them could have ceased to exist in that moment; there was only him.

She ran the hand that wasn't gripping his shirt through his hair, fingers tangling in the dark locks and tightening just enough to pull as he turned them, pushing her back against the edge of the table. Mya broke the kiss, gasping.

"*Mya*," Kayden growled, voice wrecked with wanting. He pressed kisses against her jaw, her throat, refusing to let go. He tried to reconnect their lips but she turned away and he groaned, low in his throat.

"Kayden," Mya gasped. "Just—Ah—Wait a moment."

Their plates were still sitting on the table, and she shoved them and the remaining food out of the way, clutching at his shoulders as he suddenly lifted her, setting her where they had been.

And then it was over.

She was back in the room with its mess and the rotten egg smell of sulfur, and the man who had rescued her was looking down at her as though he wasn't quite sure whether she was entirely all there or not.

Mya felt heat bloom across her face at the memory she had just experienced, if it was a memory, and was grateful for the darkness of the room that hid it from his sight. She took a shaky breath.

"Are you..." If it was the wrong question, he might be angry, but it was one that she had to ask. If she had remembered such things about him, then he must be something to her. Someone important. "Are you my husband?"

He shook his head. She saw the motion of it against the darkness. When he smiled, his teeth were white in the dim light that trickled through the doorway. "No," he said, the deep timbre of his voice sending a pleasant little shudder through her. Nothing at all like the fear that the other man had woken. "I'm not."

At least he wasn't angry. He sounded more amused than anything, as though there were laughter hiding just inside the words. It was that laughter that gave Mya the boldness to continue on in her questioning.

"A lover, perhaps?"

This time, the laughter slipped free of the hold he'd had on it, and echoed in the room. Mya liked it, the way that it filled up the space between them, warm and uninhibited. There was something pleasantly familiar about that as well. Something that felt like security. Like home.

"No," he said. "Not that either, I'm afraid. Where are you getting such notions, my lady?"

"I..." The heat in Mya's cheeks deepened. "It's nothing. Only that you were here to save me and I thought maybe you knew who I was. There's something about you that seems so very familiar. As though I've seen you before."

"Not as far as I can tell," the man said, grunting as he lifted himself from his knees with her weight in his arms. Mya clung to him, afraid to fall, and the embrace tightened just a little, steady and strong. He walked carefully, keeping his steps even so that the motion wouldn't jostle her. "See as, far as I can tell, I've never seen you before in my life, lass."

Chapter 4

How could he feel so familiar when he had never seen her before? Mya tried, as he carried her through the wreckage, to understand it. He looked down at her as though she was a stranger, but she had never felt anything as safe as his arms around her. Had never felt so surely as though she belonged somewhere.

Then again, she thought, with a little internal laugh, she couldn't remember ever feeling safe. In the mere moments since she had woken in that house with the sounds of a war raging around her, how could she have? Maybe it was just that. Just that he was the first thing that she had since she had found herself there that had not been out to kill her. But that didn't explain that way that she looked into his eyes and saw home, or the way that the strength of his arms holding her felt like a place she had been before. Perhaps he simply reminded her of someone she had once known—of the lover that she was sure she had left behind somewhere, wondering what had become of her. Why had she left him? Had they been separated by the war? Was he a soldier too, and it was only the uniform that made her feel as though the man holding her had been a part of her since before she could even recall?

He stepped over something laying in their path, made a sound through his teeth as his foot came down that Mya was sure was a sound of pain. She remembered the way that he had held his hand to his side when he had first turned away from the man on the ground. He was hurt, and he was still trying to carry her through a war zone.

"I can walk," Mya said, unwrapping her arms from around his shoulders and moving like she would stand on her own feet. The man holding her didn't let go.

"No," he said. "You aren't well enough to walk, and I can't let you slow us down. We're putting our lives on the line here already. It's better if I just carry you."

Mya shook her head. "You're hurt," she said. "I know that you are. Carrying me can't be doing anything good for your wound. I can keep up. Just put me down."

"I won't."

There was hardly any arguing with that. When she struggled, he simply tightened his arms around her, and she sighed and slumped back into his arms, trying to ignore the way that her head pounded. To their left, something struck ground and the whole area shook. Mya turned her face against her rescuer's shoulder to block out the white-hot light that burned across her vision, but there was no ignoring the noise of it, and the ache in her head redoubled.

"We're going to get you to a doctor," the man's deep voice murmured above her. "Just a few moments longer."

He needed to get to a doctor too. Mya tried to convince herself to make one last bid for freedom, but the ache in her head was making the world spin, and in truth she wasn't sure that she wouldn't immediately fall on her backside should he actually agree to set her on her feet.

The sounds of the bombs receded behind them as they moved deeper into the town that the man had been walking toward. May dared to lift her head. On either side she saw buildings going by, all of them dark and shuttered tight. The inhabitants gone, or simply awaiting the end of the shelling? When she looked up, she saw dark, winged shapes gliding overhead in menacing formation, the drone of them audible under the periodic rumblings of the explosives they dropped.

How had this come to pass? She could not, for the life of her, recall anything of the sort. Had she lost her memory so completely? It didn't seem possible, when she could remember her own name, could remember the names things around her were called. If she had forgotten entirely, she wouldn't know what a chair was. Or a bomb. Or a soldier.

"H-Here," the man huffed.

He was carrying her across a wide green expanse of lawn, dotted here and there with trees, and up ahead there was a large square-ish building of pale stone, with a tower at one end. The windows glowed red and gold in the light of the fire from the buildings in the distance.

"Where are we?" Mya asked, staring at the building.

"The emergency hospital," he said. "It's not actually one, of course, but we'll take anything we can get these days, and the nuns have been kind in sharing the space."

A convent. Mya tipped her head back to follow the lines of the walls toward the cloudy, plane-filled sky as they stepped beneath them. Someone held the door open, and then they were inside, sound and fire closed off behind them. She took a breath of air that was almost clean. Up ahead, someone was hurrying along the hall, but Mya caught only a glimpse of a uniform.

"Doctor," the man was saying above her. "We need a doctor."

They were ushered into a room where a man in a white coat stood. He turned toward them at the sound of the door, and frowned when he saw Mya. "What is this?"

"Lieutenant Kayden McGregor. Highland regiment," the man said. "I found her in one of the buildings out there, on the wrong end of a German soldier's gun."

"She doesn't look shot," the doctor said. His accent, Mya noted, was French.

"No," Kayden said, and even the name was familiar. She could swear she had heard it before, could almost imagine the way it would taste on her tongue. "She has a head injury, I think."

"And your wound?" The doctor said as Kayden laid Mya down in the empty bed.

"It's nothing, Sir. He grazed me with a bullet. I'll be just fine."

"You'll be sitting right down there and letting me have a look at you, is what you'll be doing," the doctor said firmly. "Do not leave here, and I mean it."

Kayden sighed, and dropped down to sit in a chair that took up one corner of the room.

It was not, Mya realized as she looked around at the desk in the corner piled high with papers and reports, one of the rooms for the enlisted men who had been brought in to the hospital. The room must be the doctor's own, and she wondered why she'd been brought there, before she realized that they could hardly have a woman sharing common space with a bunch of soldiers. But weren't there rooms for the nuns? Or a separate room that she could be put in? Maybe they were just that full of patients, and Mya wondered how badly the war she seemed to have stumbled into was going. Or maybe it was only that it had been the closest bed, and the doctor already in the room. She couldn't tell.

The doctor leaned over her, his face filling up her vision. He was an older gentleman, with salt and pepper streaks in his dark hair, and kind blue eyes.

"I'm going to take a look at you now," he said. "Let me know if anything I'm doing hurts, *S'il vous plaît*."

Mya nodded. He pulled out a light, and shone it into her eyes, and Mya blinked against the brilliance of it, trying to ignore the lance of pain that it sent through her skull.

When he backed up, he was shaking his head. "Your head hurts, *oui*?"

"Yes," Mya said. "Very much."

He hmmed to himself and ran his fingers carefully over her scalp, pausing when he found the tender place that made her hiss through her teeth with pain.

"You've certainly hit it hard. It seems you have a concussion, though you are lucky it is nothing worse. If your brain were bleeding, we would not be able to do much for you so far out into the battle zone." He straightened, turning to look at Kayden, who was slumped over on the chair. "It's obvious that you're injured as well. We have not yet had nurses brought in. The nuns are doing the best they can, but I cannot pull them off any of the severely injured men, so you'll need to stay with her and make certain that she remains awake for a time. If she drifts off to sleep, there's a chance she will not wake up."

Kayden nodded, and the doctor called someone from the hall outside, who picked Mya up in his arms the same way Kayden had, and carried her down the hall to another empty room where there were four beds set up against the walls. It was small enough that they hardly fit, and Mya wondered how they planned on moving men in and out of them, or getting nurses around them to tend to the wounded.

"Here," the doctor said.

The man carrying Mya laid her down, and she gratefully let her head rest against the softness of a pillow once more. Her eyelids felt heavy, trying to drag themselves downward.

"Ah-ah," the doctor scolded, snapping his fingers in front of her face. "Wake up. You cannot fall asleep just yet, unfortunately."

Kayden had sat down on the bed next to hers, and the doctor turned briskly away to look at his wound.

Mya could see it now, the spreading stain of blood on the right side of his uniform shirt, just under his ribs. The doctor caught the hem of the shirt and pulled it up, and she felt her cheeks growing warm, knowing that it was likely proper for her to look away, and not quite able to bring herself to. Her eyes traced the lines of the muscle in Kayden's abs, and if she hadn't been feeling so poorly she thought that she might have had a little more reaction to the sight. Kayden glanced over and caught her staring, and the slight heat in her face flared to almost painful red. She looked quickly away, trying to ignore the sound of his quiet chuckle.

"The bullet went through and through," the doctor said. "We will stitch it up and you'll be quite healed in a few days. If we had more pain medication, I would offer you some, but we're waiting on the next shipment, and for minor wounds like these..."

"I don't need medication," Kayden said. "Go on with it. I'll be fine."

Mya looked up again as the doctor threaded his needle. Kayden was watching the work, and she saw his jaw tighten until a muscle jumped under the skin when the needle went in. She winced sympathetically at the imagined sting. At least the man was good at his work; it was only a matter of moments before he was tying off the stitches and wiping the blood from the site of the wound. Kayden hadn't made a sound.

"It would do you well to lie down," he told Kayden. "And rest. Do not sleep, though, *s'il vous plaît*. You will need to keep Miss..." At that, he seemed to realize that he hadn't yet asked her name and turned around to look at her with a question in his expression.

"Mya," she said, searching her memory for the surname. "Mya..."

The doctor's forehead creased in a frown, and he bustled quickly away from Kayden to lean over her bedside once more. "Do you not remember your name?"

She took a deep breath and reached back, trying to find it. It had to be there somewhere. "Boyle," she said finally, almost wanting to snap her fingers. "My name is Mya Boyle."

"But you had trouble recalling it?" The doctor prompted.

"I can't remember anything more than that," Mya confessed. "I have no idea how I found myself in the building that Kayden took me out of, or where I was before tonight."

"That is quite concerning. We'll certainly have to keep you for observation." He looked at her sternly. "It is more imperative than ever that you not fall asleep, Miss Boyle. Such memory loss is likely a sign of quite serious damage to your brain. Lieutenant McGregor will be here to help you stay awake, but it will be better for you and easier for him if you are making an effort. Can you do that, mademoiselle?"

Mya nodded. "I can stay awake," she said, despite the fact that it seemed all her body wanted was sleep.

"Good. See that you do. And see that you help her keep that promise," he added in Kayden's direction before hurrying out of the room.

"Thank you," Mya said when he was gone, turning to look at the pale man who was still sitting on the edge of the other bed. "For rescuing me."

"I could hardly do anything else and consider myself a good man," Kayden said, looking up from the hands that were folded in his lap to smile at her. The sight of it made Mya's heart skip a beat in her chest and took her breath away. "Though I have to wonder what a Scottish woman was doing so far from home in the middle of a war zone."

"Should I be wondering the same thing about you, then?" Mya asked, because she couldn't answer his question. "You're a Scotsman, in a war zone, far from home."

"I'm a soldier," Kayden said, looking at her again with that expression that said he wasn't sure he was all there. Maybe she wasn't. She had hit her head rather hard, after all. "I'm here with the army. Trying to stop this damned war before it gets any worse. We're being bombed back home too. Whole cities burning. It can't go on."

He sighed, running a hand through the hair that Mya somehow was sure had been longer, she could picture it clearly. Though she could not remember ever seeing him before that night except in the misty way that one remembered dreams. Why was it that she knew him, she wondered again? Why was it that he was the only thing that seemed to connect?

"This is a bad war, Miss Boyle. As bad as the Great War. Maybe worse. They're aiming to take over as much of the world as they can get their hands on, and we have to stop them before they do."

The Great War. Mya didn't know the name, but of course she wouldn't. She could see on Kayden's face that he had realized she didn't.

"There was another war. As big as this one. I wasn't around for it, but they thought that after it was over, that would be the end of it." He shook his head. "They were wrong."

"Then you're doing the right thing," Mya said. The best sat close enough side by side that she could reach out and brush her fingers over his, and after a moment of startled immobility he met the touch and took her hand, looking down at her with an intensity in his dark eyes that she couldn't quite read. "You're going to stop them this time."

He smiled, but it wasn't the bright, sure thing of a moment ago. It was only a pale, faltering echo. "I hope so," he said. "I truly do hope so, Miss Boyle."

Chapter 5

The sound of footsteps outside pulled them apart, and Kayden dropped Mya's hand back to the blankets, laying his own once more in his lap. The doctor stepped into the room and looked them both over as though he felt he was missing something, but Kayden's expression gave nothing away, and Mya hoped there was nothing in hers that could be read. She supposed, if there was ever a time to hold hands with a strange man, this was it, but still some part of her didn't want the doctor knowing. Didn't want the private moment between them shared with someone else.

"Lieutenant McGregor," he said sternly. "You really ought to lie down."

Kayden looked for a moment like he would argue, but then he glanced at Mya and sighed, pulling aside the blankets and sliding beneath them without bothering to take off his uniform, though he did pause to unlace his boots and pull them from his feet, setting them beside the bed post.

"Now," the doctor said. "As I mentioned before, both of you will need to stay here and rest. I will check in on you when I have time, but I cannot guarantee when that will be with everything that's going on here. So I will rely on you to take care of yourselves as much as possible. That means, Lieutenant, do not let Miss Boyle fall asleep. And Miss Boyle, if you could at least attempt to see that the Lieutenant remains in bed and resting, I would deeply appreciate it."

Mya wasn't entirely sure that anyone could keep the man in bed when he didn't want to be, but she didn't think the doctor needed to be told that. Judging by the look on his face, he was well aware of just what kind of patient he had on his hands.

"I'll watch over her," Kayden said. He flashed a smile at Mya. "Someone needs to make sure that she isn't a spy."

"A spy? I—" She realized then that he was laughing silently at her, his dark eyes dancing with it, and cut herself abruptly off, not giving him the satisfaction of finishing her retort.

"I hardly think Miss Boyle is in any shape to be spying on anyone, though I suppose if she does attempt anything you're more than equipped to handle her," the doctor said dryly. "I shall be back, or send one of my assistants, in the morning. If you need anything before then, simply call out, and someone will come to check that you are well. One of the nuns ought to be by with some food and water for the two of you later." He scratched his head. "I'm just not sure when."

"Thank you," Mya said, and the doctor smiled at her.

"Of course," he said. "It is, after all, what we do here. Even in the middle of such a war, we help those we can."

And then he was gone again, and it was Mya and Kayden alone once more.

For a long moment, they were both quiet, staring up at the ceiling. There was a crack in the plaster, and Mya followed it from the corner where it started out into the middle of the room, wandering absently if it had been there before the bombing started, or if there was a chance the whole place would come down on their heads with a few more good shakes. She wished she hadn't had that thought. "Where are you from?" she asked quietly, to distract herself, rolling onto her side to look at Kayden.

"Scotland," he said.

Mya scowled at him. "I think you know what I mean," she said. "I'm well aware of your country of origin. But tell me more about your hometown? I have to stay awake somehow."

It seemed that appealing to his sense of honor worked, because he sighed and turned to face, her, leaning up on one elbow. "I'm from Inverness," he said and then paused. "Do you know where that is?"

Mya knew Scotland, or the highlands. She was sure she did. Except she couldn't seem to remember any cities or anything. If she spoke like him, she had to be from somewhere. Maybe his explaining would trigger a memory. "I don't... remember."

"It's a city at the southern edge of the highlands. We're a bit west of Loch Ness, if you have heard of it. Famous for—" he paused, obviously remembering once more that even if she had heard of it she likely wouldn't remember. "Never mind. It does not matter."

"No," Mya said. "Tell me? Famous for what?"

Kayden chuckled. "Very well, then. They say there is a monster in it."

Mya stared at him. "A monster? Truly?" Her eyes narrowed. "Are you trying to trick me into believing something because I cannot remember any of my history, because if you are that would be a dirty trick."

"No, no," Kayden said. "I'm not trying to trick you at all. They truly do say there's a monster in the lake. A great beast, that comes in the night and carries off sheep. And occasionally a lovely young lass or two. Though Inverness is far enough from it that we don't have to worry."

"Now I know you're trying to trick me," Mya said with a smile and then turned serious. "I'll have you know that I think it's very rude to lie to a woman in convalescence."

That brought outright laughter from him. "You cannot be too far gone if you are using such big words, Miss Boyle."

"I'm on death's door," Mya snapped, but she couldn't keep a straight face as she said it.

"Oh, indeed. I can see it in your face. One foot in the grave, you are."

"In which case," Mya said. "You should tell me more about your home. To comfort me on my death bed."

"Should I now?"

She simply looked at him, silent and waiting, and he shook his head and went on.

"I live in a wee house in the hills, above the city. It's a little cleaner there. A little quieter." His voice softened. "Behind the house, the moors climb farther into the highlands, all purple with heather in the summer. Full of midges trying to eat you alive, and great fat bees buzzing about. It's cloudy more often than not, but I don't mind that. Windy days keep the midges away, at least."

Mya, eyes slipping almost closed, could imagine the place as he described it. She saw in her mind's eye the dream that she had been woken from by the thunder of the bombs, the hills rolling toward the horizon, and down below, before the lights of the city, the silver gleam of the water that cut them off from the town.

"There is a firth there. An inlet from the sea. It lies between the moors and Inverness, and at night the moon shines on the water and lights it up like a mirror."

Yes, Mya thought, reaching for the images that came with his words. Those green hills felt like home. She knew them with ache behind her breastbone like a pull toward the distant highlands, and wondered if perhaps that was how she knew the man before her. If they had both come from the same place. But he had said he did not know her, and so she couldn't be sure. Was he lying? Were they both wrong? Perhaps she remembered fantasies only, and he had never bothered to see her, though she had noticed him. How large a town, she wondered, was Inverness?

"Miss Boyle!"

It was only as his voice growled her name that Mya realized her eyes had been closed and she had been drifting somewhere between sleep and waking, and that Kayden had been calling her name.

Her eyelids snapped open. "I'm sorry," she said. "I didn't realize I was falling asleep."

"You've nothing to apologize for. But the doctor did ask me to keep an eye on you, and that's what I intend to do."

Mya sat up in bed, propping the pillows behind her so that it was not too much trouble to remain semi-upright. Her head still ached, but the quiet flow of words had soothed the pounding of it somewhat. "Do you miss it?" she asked finally.

Kayden's eyebrows lifted. "Miss what? Inverness?"

"Your home. Amidst all this. It seems as though it would be something to miss."

He swallowed, and her eyes followed the motion of his throat. "Yes," he said, lifting his eyes to hers. "I do miss it. Especially here. But that's the very reason why I'm here. To save it. I will not let it become like this place."

Mya, thinking of the little house, ruined and alone, and the burning from the bombs, nodded. She could not imagine the place he described becoming what she had seen of the landscape outside. Buildings fallen down and grass scorched black. Water choked with wreckage.

"I hope it never becomes that," she whispered He might have answered, but just then one of the nuns entered with a tray of food. She smiled at them both as she set it down at the foot of Mya's bed and handed a plate to each of them. Glasses filled with water went on the small table that sat between their beds.

"Thank you," Mya said as she turned away, and she paused, turning back to them.

"Yes," Kayden said. "Thank you. *Merci.*"

"*De rein.* You're welcome." She smiled a benevolent smile and bustled out again. Kayden watched her go with a thoughtful expression on his face.

"I wish I could remember mine," Mya said softly. "My home. I feel as though... When you describe your home, it sounds familiar to me. Like a place I've been before. Like a place that I miss, or

want to return to. But I don't know if that's because it's a place
I've actually been, or if I just want to have what you're
describing."

She set the plate the nun had handed her on the table, not
sure she was hungry. Her head still ached, and the pain of it made
her stomach turn.

Kayden watched her like he knew, and after a moment he sat
up and slid out from the under the blankets.

"Where are you going?" Mya asked.

"To see if they can find something to give you for the pain."

Mya shook her head. "He told you when we came in; they
don't have anything. I'm not going to take medicine from
soldiers that need it. I'll be okay."

Kayden, already half way to the door, turned around and
looked at her, then came back to sit on the side of the bed,
looking down at her. "You shouldn't have to lie there in pain."

"And neither should the soldiers who are fighting and dying
in this war. My headache will pass. Besides," she added, trying to
find a smile to go with the words. "It keeps me awake. So I
suppose that's a plus."

Kayden shook his head. "You're a brave woman, Mya Boyle."

"No," Mya said. "I'm just a decent person. Anyone else in my
position would do the same thing."

"I'm not so sure of that," Kayden said.

He was leaning over her, his eyes on her face. Mya wondered
what it was that he looked for there. She wondered if he found it.

"Kayden," she said, voice soft. She didn't know what she
intended to say after that. The question never left her lips.

His hand stroked over her cheek, and for a flickering instant
she saw him in another time, another place, his fingers brushing
against her cheek. She took a breath and forgot to let it out again
as he leaned down. His lips met hers.

Mya breathed in the scent of him, so strangely familiar, and
arched up into the kiss. His arm slid under her shoulders to

support the weight of her body. For the space of a moment, nothing existed but the two of them, sharing breath and space between them. Mya's eyelids fluttered closed.

Too soon, the kiss broke. Kayden leaned back, and then he was up and moving, taking a seat on his own bed before Mya had time to even reach for him. She watched him across the sudden distance, her hand lifting to her mouth as though it had a will of its own.

"I'm sorry," he said. "I shouldn't have done that. It was inappropriate."

"I hardly minded."

Kayden's eyes lifted to hers. "No?"

Mya laughed. "No. I can assure you there are worse things than being kissed by a handsome soldier."

His eyebrows rose toward his hairline, the corners of his mouth tipping up. "Handsome, am I?"

"Don't fish for compliments," Mya admonished, a smile trying to slip through the words. "It isn't seemly."

"You're entirely different kind of woman," Kayden said, chuckling. "And I think I like it." He picked up the plate of food that was sitting on his side of the table and started eating the already cold food.

"Entirely different from what, exactly?" Mya asked, hiding her laughter, and letting him worry whether or not he'd just offended her.

He paused, fork halfway to his mouth and his eyes darted to her, and then back to his plate. "Och, well, you've opinions of your own, and you're not afraid to state them." He took the mouthful of food from the fork, and chewed it slowly, contemplating his answer. "You're not so packed full of airs and graces that it's impossible to know what to say to you. And you've a sense of humor. Which," he held the fork up between them as though staving off anything she might be about to say, "I'm not for one moment implying is rare amongst the fairer sex, but yours is," he stabbed his fork into his food again, then raised his eyes to her again, "Accessible. There's something easygoing to your nature." He made a slightly dismissive gesture with his fork. "I'm not sure I'm saying this very well. There's something to you that's..."

"Familiar?" She offered, when he paused again, searching for the right word.

His answering nod wasn't as much agreement as concession. "Aye," he said softly, after a moment. "Familiar."

Maybe it's because we're both Scottish, Mya wondered. *Or maybe it's something more?*

Chapter 6

The doctor returned quite a few hours later to check in on Mya, and declared that if she had showed no further symptoms, a little sleep was not likely to do her any harm. Mya, whose eyes kept trying to close on their own, was grateful for the reprieve. She let herself sink a little deeper into the mattress, pulling the blanket up warm around her chin, and stole a last glance at Kayden, who looked as though he was on the verge of falling asleep himself. Her lips still tingled with their kiss.

She supposed he'd had reason to be a bit concerned that she might take offense, after all. It had been rather quick. But she didn't feel that way about it. When they'd kissed, it hadn't felt like something rushed or impatient. It had felt like something that was meant to happen. Something they had both been waiting for. The way Mya felt as though she'd been waiting for Kayden since before she could remember. She couldn't explain why, but there was just something about him, she thought as she drifted off into dreams. Just something about him.

"I have something for you," a voice she recognized as Kayden's said behind her.

Mya paused, fingers loosening on the string of the bow she held to allow it to slowly straighten, tension leaving it. "Something that cannot wait until I'm finished with the shot?"

Beyond the target set up at the far end of the makeshift range, the hills stacked one on the other, rolling up from the moors to the blue sky, green and peaceful in the sunlight.

"I think you'll want to see this first."

Letting the tip of the arrow sag toward the ground so that she wasn't pointing it at Kayden, Mya turned.

He was holding a bow. It was obviously brand new, made of some gleaming, golden wood that had been well-oiled recently. The string was taut and fresh, without any wear. In his other hand, he held a leather quiver full of arrows. She stared at him with wide eyes as he lifted his hands, obviously offering them to her.

"Where did you..." Mya un-nocked the arrow from the string and slid it back into the borrowed quiver on her back, holding the bow she'd been using in one hand. "Where did you get that?"

"The bow I made," Kayden said. The smooth sheen on the wood said that he'd sanded it well. He had obviously taken great care in the making. "And the arrows and quiver I picked up in town. I thought you ought to have your own. They needed to be matched to the draw of the bow anyway, and you can't have arrows without something to carry them about in."

Mya stepped sideways to lean the bow she had been using against the wall of the little stone house that stood off the side, the quiver with it, and then reached out for the bow that Kayden held. He passed it across the small space between them, and Mya took it in her hands, running her fingers over the graceful curve. The wood was as smooth as it had looked.

"This is beautiful," she breathed. "Kayden. I don't know how to thank you."

He reached one hand up to rub at the back of his neck, a crooked smile on his face. "You needn't. It was just a practicality. Bows are simple enough to make, anyway."

And then the bow was gone.

And he was gone.

The hills faded into an empty room with wallpaper of gold damask, food and drinks set out on tables at its far end. Mya moved through the room, the skirts she wore whispering around her, and helped herself to a few of the cookies that sat out on the table, nibbling at one with powdered sugar dusted over the top of it. It was better than she had expected. She finished it quickly, and the second cookie followed right after. She was reaching for a third when she heard the sound of footsteps coming down the hall and she felt suddenly guilty, as though she had done something wrong. Someone would get in trouble, she thought, if she was caught there. Not just her, but the people who had brought her with them to this place. She could not recall their names, only that there was a sense of friendship wrapped up with them. That she cared for them. She ducked back against the wall beside the open door and hoped that the sounds were just one of the servants going about his business, and that his business didn't include the room she was in.

Of course she had no such luck. But she had already known, somehow, that she wouldn't.

The footsteps turned, and entered, and belonged, as she had expected, to Kayden. Blessedly, he had not yet seen her, his back still to the door and her little corner, and Mya tried to edge silently out of the room before he turned. But of course she had only managed half the distance, despite her straining, feeling as though she was moving through molasses, when Kayden spun to face her, his eyebrows lifting.

"Are you hiding from me now?" he asked, laughter at the edges of the words.

"Not in the slightest," Mya snapped back, brushing imaginary wrinkles from her skirt with both gloved hands. The words came from her mouth as though she had said them before. "I simply thought I would remove myself from the room before I was required to engage in further conversation with you."

"Am I truly that terrible? That you will not even speak to me?"

He sounded genuinely concerned, and Mya wondered what it was that had caused the rift between them that seemed to exist here. Why were they fighting? She took a breath, opening her mouth to speak, and closed it again. "No," she said finally. "It's not that. I was concerned about breaking rules by being in the hall alone. I would not want to get Lottie and Eleanora in trouble with the hosts."

Lottie and Eleanora. Those were the names. The friends she had not been able to quite recall.

"I'm not sure being in the hall alone with me is any better," Kayden said. He smiled, his dark eyes warm in a way that made Mya's knees feel like one of the partially melted ices sitting on the table. "In truth, I think it may be worse, as far as the hosts are concerned."

He took a step forward, toward her, and Mya took a breath she forgot to let out again. She didn't like him, she reminded the part of herself that was melting into want at his approach. He was arrogant. And condescending. And the fact that he was absolutely gorgeous did not change any of that. It didn't.

But when he closed the last distance between them and brushed the backs of his knuckles tenderly over the curve of her cheek, Mya didn't pull away. She leaned into the touch, breath escaping on a sigh.

The touch felt so strangely familiar. So perfectly right.

He leaned down and kissed her, and Mya forgot her objections about his character entirely.

Voices in the hall made them startle apart an instant later, Mya's cheeks burning red as a signal light. Anyone who walked into the room in that moment was going to know exactly what had happened. They might as well have shouted it. But no one came in. The footsteps receded onward down the hall, and Mya slipped out the door and back toward the noise of the ball before Kayden could stop her.

The world around her receded.

Mist drifted in, hiding hall and carpet, and through it she caught glimpses of green hills and the trunks of trees. Half-seen images that she could not quite make out. Herself, dancing in Kayden's arms. A flash of white hide, and a graceful, four-legged form bounding away. And then nothing but darkness.

She woke, momentarily disorientated and startled, unsure of where she was or what it was that had woken her.

"Ah, Miss Boyle." There was a man standing in the doorway, one hand raised as though he had just knocked on the frame. "Do you mind if I come in for a moment? I have some supplies for you." He looked down to where his other hand appeared to be holding a small pile of clothes, pressed against his chest to steady them.

"No," Mya said, still confused, not recognizing the man. "I mean, of course I don't mind. Please come in." She sat up in the bed and pulled herself more fully awake, glad that she was still dressed.

"I'm afraid that we have nothing for women in our supplies," he said as he moved forward and set the small stack of clothing down on the bed.

The doctor slipped in a moment. "Let me just check your head." He flashed a light into her eyes and touched her head, checking for injury or issues. Satisfied with his inspection he nodded at the clothes. "Glad they found you some." The doctor nodded at the man standing by the wall before leaving again.

The man cleared his throat. "If you wish something of that nature, then you'll have to find it for yourself, though from what I understand you are not to be out of bed for some time yet. I can offer you things that will keep you warm, at least. They are comfortable enough, clean, and in good repair. For anything else you might try asking the nuns."

Mya leaned over to see what items he'd brought her. There was a thick sweater sitting on top, and beneath that a pair of black button up shirts. Two sets of trousers, one in black and one in dark green. There also proved to be socks. Nothing that she would have chosen to wear, but as he said, they would keep her warm. Though, stealing a glance at Kayden, Mya wondered what he would think of her in them, and then admonished herself for worrying about it. They were good, sturdy clothes, and she was in the middle of a war. She should hardly be thinking about whether or not her attire would attract Kayden's gaze.

"Thank you," she said, touching the clothing, "it was very thoughtful of you."

"It is no trouble at all, miss, I assure you. Though I do have an assistant who ought to be bringing the rest of your things. Lazy bloody—" He cut himself off, apparently remembering that he was in the presence of a woman, and marched out into the hall to return with a skinny young man who was carrying a small trunk by the handles at each end.

"The chest's a bit broken. Not badly. It's just the hinges," the man in charge said. "It doesn't close properly, so it can't be used by the men. But as long as you're not kicking it around or moving it too much, it should be good enough for you to keep your things in. And we've a pair of boots for you in there as well."

His assistant pulled them out and set them on the floor as he spoke. Mya hardly got more than a glimpse of them, but she could see that they were great, heavy things, and likely too big.

The man must have seen her expression, because he smiled a little ruefully as his assistant scurried out again. "We didn't have anything in women's sizes, so we got you the smallest I could find. You should be okay in them, with maybe an extra pair of socks. Like I always say to the men, look after your feet, because they look after you. Important things, feet."

He glanced down at the shoes that were sitting by the foot of the bed, the ones that she had worn from the house where

Kayden found her. They weren't exactly practical, but he didn't point that out. Didn't say anything about them at all. Mya was grateful.

"Oh, and..." he paused, as though he wasn't quite sure how to carry on, and glanced over at Kayden, who was still soundly sleeping, "I did manage to obtain some things of, er, rather more delicate nature. They were sent to us by mistake, and, well, I'm just glad that you can make use of them. They're tucked into the trousers. Didn't want any of the men seeing them and getting the wrong idea."

Mya, wondering what could send him into such a state—he was actually blushing, for heaven's sake—glanced inside the trousers and had to stifle a laugh. Tucked into them were half a dozen pairs of women's underwear. She set the trousers back down and gave him the sweetest smile she could muster. "Thank you. Mr..."

"Ah. Corporal Hartle. I'm the quartermaster here. So if you need anything, just come talk to me and I'll see what I can do about it, though I can't promise you any indulgences that we don't allow the men, I'm afraid. Just wouldn't do well for morale."

"Of course," Mya said. "I understand. Thank you."

"Have a nice night, miss."

He turned smartly on his heel and walked away then, obviously grateful to be both rid of the undergarments that he'd brought her as well as out of her presence. Mya giggled a little as she pulled the underwear out and folded them, putting them with the rest of the things in the chest. The Corporal hadn't been lying about it being broken. She lifted the lid experimentally and it opened somewhat lopsidedly. It closed a little lopsidedly, too, so the ends of the catch didn't quite line up with one another which meant that it couldn't be fastened or locked, but at least it did close. It was sturdy enough, and perfect for her needs. And, she thought, smiling again, she wouldn't need a lock. It was very unlikely that anyone would be coming to make off with her underwear.

That done, she crawled back into bed to rest her head against the pillow. It seemed that things were going to turn out alright after all, she thought, looking up at the ceiling and the sculpted plaster around the light rose. Whatever else happened, at least they were kind to her, and she had things that would keep her safe from the elements if she was forced to venture outdoors. There were, she decided, certainly worse situations to be in.

Chapter 7

Kayden still slept, his chest rising and falling evenly in the light that spilled in through the windows and under the door. Mya rolled onto her side, watching him in silence.

Why did she dream of his face?

It would make sense if they were simply dreams. He had rescued her, after all, of course her mind would pull from events so recent. But they were not the sort of jumbled memories of the day that one expected. They were seemingly memories from long before her rescue. And yet, how could they be memory, when they did not match up with each other? They made no more sense side by side than they did apart. In what world would she have learned the use of a bow and arrow barefoot in the hills, and then found herself arguing with Kayden at a party in a ball gown? Perhaps it was just a consequence of hitting her head. It had caused some sort of confusion between memory and dream, thrown them together and she could not tell the difference. Perhaps one memory was true and the other was not. Maybe she saw Kayden's face where another's should be?

She sighed, and shifted again, onto her back, sitting up against the pillows and reaching for the glass of water that had been left. She had a few days still, likely, before the doctor would declare her well enough to be on her own, but what was she to do when the time came? She had no family, no friends, no memory of who she was. Perhaps her memories would come back before then, but if they did not, she was simply stranded in a war-torn nation with no idea of where home was or how to get back to it.

Mya took a sip of water, feeling it run cool over her tongue and sooth the dry ache in her throat. Whatever happened, she would just have make it through. She would not be the only one searching for a new home. Would not be the only person who had lost family. In war time, her story was hardly unique, she was sure.

On the other bed, Kayden stirred. Mya heard the rustle of blankets and glanced over to find him shifting uneasily, his brow creased in a frown. She set the water she was holding back on the table and watched him, wondering what riled him in his dreams. His hands curled into fists against the blankets that covered him.

Should she wake him? But she didn't know him well. What if he didn't wake easily, or woke violently, expecting an enemy? Could his dreams be of the battlefield? What if he did not wish her to wake him at all? He might be embarrassed to know that she had seen him in the midst of a nightmare. She settled back against the pillows and decided to wait it out.

He grew worse. The shifting became twitches and jerks. His neck strained, as though he reached for something. Or ran from something. Mya watched for a few more moments, hoping that the dream would quiet itself and let him settle back into sleep, but he only became more agitated. When he cried out something she could understand in a hoarse whisper, Mya carefully untangled herself from her sheets and padded across the little space between them to lay a hand on his shoulder.

"Kayden?" Her voice was soft, hardly more than a whisper. "Kayden, you're having a nightmare. Wake up."

A dizzying sense that they had done this before hit her. She had woken him, before, from a nightmare, though she could not remember when or where. The sense passed as quickly as it had come, and Mya found herself looking down at the man in the bed once more, her efforts to wake him completely unsuccessfully.

"Kayden," she said again, louder. "Kayden, wake up! You're dreaming."

He jolted half upright, his hand moving to catch her wrist almost before his eyes had opened, but when he saw her standing there he dropped it back to the mattress, chest heaving with quick breaths.

"You were dreaming," Mya whispered.

Kayden sighed, and settled back into the pillow. "Yes," he said, voice rough. "I suppose I was. Thank you."

That was a dismissal, Mya knew. But she couldn't quite make herself obey it. Instead, she sat down carefully on the edge of his bed, looking down at him.

"What were you dreaming about?" she asked.

His eyes lifted to her face. He didn't answer, and Mya thought that maybe she had pushed something that he wouldn't say. But then he opened his mouth, and spoke.

"You will think it's foolish."

Mya shook her head. "No," she said. "Dreams aren't something you can control. I may not have much of a memory, but I know that much. I'm not going to laugh at you."

"I dreamed," he said and swallowed, "that I was running."

Mya leaned in a little closer, listening.

"It was good, at first. I was running through the woods, and they were green around me. I had someone by my side that I cared about. But then I..." He shook his head, looking down at his hands. "I lost her. I'm not sure how. And I tried to get to her. I knew something terrible would happen to her. But I couldn't reach her in time."

Startled, Mya thought of her own dream. The one where she was bounding through the forest, a lover at her side, and then she faltered and fell as she tried to reach him. She couldn't get to him.

"I have a dream like that," she said quietly.

Kayden looked up at her, startled. "Like the one I just described to you?"

Mya nodded. "One where I'm running. And then the person beside me is gone, and it's storming. Thunder and lightning.

Water crashing on the shore. I try to reach him, but this—this pain hits me. Like nothing I've ever felt before. It strikes me through the heart and I fall."

He was staring. Mya, a little self-conscious, curled closer in on herself, not sure if she should have told him about what she dreamed.

"That's exactly how mine ends," he said. "Or near enough."

"We're having the same dream?"

"Close to. Which... makes no sense. We don't even know each other. Why would we be sharing dreams?"

Mya lifted one shoulder in a shrug and let it fall. "Maybe it's just because we're in the same room?"

"I've had the dream before," Kayden said, shaking his head. "I..." He paused, looking at her. "There's something that I think I should tell you, Mya. You deserve to know, and I suppose I trust that you're telling the truth about who you are. So I should tell you."

"Tell me what?"

"That I—"

The sound of sudden gunfire outside cut him off.

Chapter 8

Mya jumped, as she always jumped.

She would never get used to the sound of gunfire, she thought, to the way the harsh staccato stutter seemed to split the night, making the hair on the back of her neck and along her forearms prickle with sudden adrenaline, sending her heart racing as though it kept time with the rapid bursts. She was still recovering both her breath and her composure, trying to settle back into her seat on the bed with an utterly feigned appearance of nonchalance, when she realized that Kayden was doing the opposite. He was out of the bed as quickly as her jump had carried her from it, but unlike hers, his movement had a sense of purpose to it. Before she had time to ask him what he thought he was doing he was running from the room. And towards the sound.

Of course he was.

Swallowing her slightly dismayed sigh, Mya pushed herself to her feet and moments later she was running lightly through one of the many stone hallways of the convent, following the sound of his echoing footsteps. They led her, as she had known they would, towards the exit, and as her eyes beat her body to the door she could see that it was still swinging closed, could hear the slight creak that its once well-oiled hinges were just beginning to develop. Like all else in the old convent building, they were being used to maximum capacity, and as no-one could spare the time or attention needed for simple maintenance work, Mya made a mental note to herself to remember to search out some oil and take care of them on the morrow.

As she did so she found herself almost, but not quite, remembering a short little rhyme that she thought she had known since her childhood. A traditional saying that warned against neglecting such tasks lest they become more complicated with the passage of time. For a moment she glimpsed it, vivid and whole, but as her mind reached for it became too insubstantial for her to grasp, elusive, as though it had settled upon the tip of her tongue. It was a random thing to come close to recollecting, but she hoped that perhaps it was a sign that more relevant pieces of information might fall into place, and like the tumblers in the mechanism of a lock, they would open the door to the mystery that was her past.

She was startled suddenly back to the present, however, as another round of shots rang out, the sounds ricocheting along the hallway and bouncing back to her from the walls, making her cringe slightly away from them as she ran.

It was only as she put her shoulder against the heavy wooden door and stumbled through it that she thought to wonder why on earth she had come chasing out here into the night. Kayden was nowhere to be seen and she hesitated, not sure if she should leave the relative safety of the convent walls. Despite the possible danger she found herself smiling. No matter how many pieces of her past were missing, she was certain she was not the type of woman suited to life within the walls of a nunnery, and when she caught a glimpse of a familiar figure running through the darkness on the far side of the road she gave chase once more, hoping that she was fleet enough to catch him before he disappeared again.

She ran, for a moment losing herself in the simple freedom of movement, in a chase that seemed as familiar as the rhyme she had almost recalled, so familiar, in fact, that it did not strike her as in the least bit odd that it should be so. She thought instead of how good it felt to feel the air upon her face, to push herself to greater speed, and for a moment she felt, rather than saw her mate, her lover, running somewhere ahead of her, and for a dizzyingly disorientating instant she thought she would come to a cliff, and that she could taste the salt tang of the sea in the air. In that instant it was as though she existed in two places at once, one here, in France, running over the rubble and the other, far away in—

The street ahead seemed to fill with noise, and she pushed all thoughts aside. She slithered to a less than dignified standstill as the rubble she had been running lightly over but a moment before twisted and slid beneath her feet. It was perhaps a combination of luck and instinct that made her duck behind the uncertain shelter of an already broken wall, putting it between her body and the falling shell, yet even so the concussion seemed to make the ground buck beneath her, and suddenly the darkness was filled with light, too bright for her to see anything but silhouettes. The twisted shapes of ruined buildings seemed to be printed upon her dazzled eyes, became all that she could see, black and white confusion, and noise, the air full of dust and grit and pieces of flying rubble.

Mya flattened herself against the wall, pressing her body to the brickwork, her hands covering her face, too late to shade her eyes from the blinding glare of the light, but keeping the shards and flakes of flying brick and stone from them. The hail of shrapnel seemed to rain endlessly, but eventually it lessened enough that she dared raise her head and look around. Behind her the convent was somehow undamaged, but ahead the street was barely recognizable. Lit by the red glow of steadily burning fires it was clear that at least two of the buildings had partly collapsed, and the walls had either disappeared or had spilled into the road. Mya could not help but look back at the convent and imagine, with a horrified shudder, what would have happened had the shell landed just a hundred yards behind her.

Her ears were still ringing, and she felt less than steady on her feet as she moved cautiously away from the wall and slowly out into the street. Dust and smoke filled the air, clogging her throat and drifting past her streaming eyes in thick clouds, as though she looked through a veil which lifted and dropped. She thought she might be in shock for it seemed as though she walked in slow motion. She felt somehow dislocated, further distanced from everything around her by the strange silence she seemed to be surrounded by, shrouded in, and she did not know if, further away, the shelling had ceased or if she was still deafened by the blast and could no longer hear it.

Kayden, she wondered, wrapping her arms tightly around her chest. She thought he had been running close by, but when she tried to remember where it was as though her thoughts stalled, and she could not take them back that far. She could see no movement amongst the rubble, except the flickering of the fires themselves. She looked wildly around, but all she could see was smoke and flames, and when she called she could not hear her own voice. Her tear-filled eyes continued to scan the wreckage of the street as she wandered dazedly down it.

She reached the first of the buildings that had collapsed, and found herself standing on a pile of rubble. The window and much of the wall nearest to her was gone, or perhaps that was what she now stood upon. It took her a long time to realize that she was looking down into a downstairs room, because even in the light from the fires it was almost too difficult to make sense of what she could see in the building, to read them as the remains of rooms for their shapes were so changed and distorted that recognizing them as what they had been was not easy. Where the ceiling would have been, the room was open to the sky, one of the walls was missing entirely, and those that remained were buckled and bowed, the windows gaping holes. And still nothing and nobody moved.

She did not know what it was that made her turn when she did. She had been peering intently down into the wreckage that had been a building less than an hour before, when she suddenly stood straight, and then looked back over her shoulder. And that was when she saw him, proud and beautiful, his head held high, standing on the rubble on what had been the far side of the road.

She turned slowly, not because she was afraid to startle the beast, but because it seemed impossible that he could be there. Just as her brain had found it difficult to make sense of what she saw in the ruined buildings, so it struggled now. Not to recognize him, for he was too obviously a stag to be mistaken for anything else, but to place him in these surroundings, to give him context within them. That was far more difficult a task.

A fire burning behind him threw him into stark relief, silhouetted him against the flames and surrounded him with a strange red glow, making him appear otherworldly and ethereal. He was utterly magnificent. The graceful sweep and curve of his antlers and the sharp points that tipped their many tines added to his majesty, and he wore them like a crown, his proud head held high. His liquid eyes shone with a fierce intelligence and he met Mya's gaze, held it calmly.

What are you doing here? she wondered, and she did not know if she had asked the words aloud or if she had spoken them silently, within the privacy of her own mind.

She did not know whether to be relieved or disappointed when he didn't answer her.

Mya was not certain how long they stood that way, looking into one another's eyes across the ruin and devastation. Moments or hours could have passed. It was as though time had stopped working, had ceased to mean anything. As though it had no place there, for there was no room for it. There was no room for anything else at all. There was only them.

And then he flicked an ear back and it was as though the spell broke. He turned his head, looking away from her, his attention going to something behind her, and Mya too turned, her eyes following the direction of his look. They were no longer alone.

She caught movement in the roadway by the convent, but no fires burned there and she could not make out who it was.

Kayden? It was not where she thought he would come from, but that didn't stop hope building in her chest.

She looked back, to the stag, but he was moving now, his long legs delicately picking his way through the rubble, and as he turned she saw the white of his sides, clean and startlingly bright.

Don't go, she wanted to call to him, but even as the thought formed she dismissed it. Where had she come by such a foolish notion? Of course he would go. What else would he do? Even so, as he began to move away she felt a pang of loss, of loneliness. And as if he could sense it he stopped mid stride, one foreleg still raised, and, turning his head he looked back to her over his shoulder. Their eyes met again, but this time it was for a moment only. Mya lifted one of her hands to give him a tiny little wave, and then, feeling self-conscious, she let it drop again just as he seemed to explode into sudden motion, leaping and bounding away. She watched him for as long as she could see him, until he disappeared between the twisted ruins on the far side of the road and melted away into the night.

Kayden, she thought again, but instead of turning to look for whoever it had been back by the convent building she found herself staring after the stag, hoping to catch one last sight of him. She could not. He was gone, swallowed by the darkness as completely as if he had never been, but still she looked, subconsciously leaning towards the place where she had seen him last.

Perhaps it was straining her eyes trying to see into the impenetrable darkness, or perhaps it was simply that she had been so distracted by the stag, now he, and the distraction were gone she was suddenly, painfully aware of how much her head hurt. Her physical state made itself known to her, coming back slowly but relentlessly. Her pounding headache leading her in turn to realize that her eyes and mouth felt as though they were filled with grit, and while her eyes watered so much that her face was wet with tears, in contrast her mouth was so dry that her tongue felt swollen, and her throat was sore and constricted. Her ears still rang, too, with a high-pitched whistling sound that changed pitch slightly when she cautiously moved her head, and then wished she had not, as everything swam alarmingly out of focus and for long, dizzy moments she thought she might fall.

"Mademoiselle?" The voice seemed to come from a very long way away, but when she turned, unsteadily, in its direction, one of the men from the hospital stood beside her. "You should not be out here, Mademoiselle. It is not safe, no?"

He turned away from her, cupping one of his hands to his mouth and calling something in French and then he offered Mya his arm. "The 'ospital?" he asked her, not pronouncing the 'h' sound at the beginning of the word.

Mya tried to answer, but her voice was a barely audible croak. She slipped her hand through his offered arm, nodding instead in an attempt to convey agreement and gratitude. The sudden head movement made her dizzy once more and she found herself leaning more heavily upon him than she had intended to. He spoke to her again, but his voice was too quiet, fading, just as everything around her seemed to be fading, receding.

There was another man, then, the one the first had called to, Mya supposed, although rational thought seemed to be one more thing that was fading from her reach. She thought she recognized him from the hospital, too, and when he spoke to her he had a different accent again.

Mya gave up trying to make sense of things, focusing instead on staying on her feet, and the two men seemed to understand, for they took one of her arms each, supporting her between them, and helping her back in the direction of the hospital, but as she let them turn her away she could not resist taking one last look in the direction the stag had gone.

She did not see the stag, but instead she saw—

Her thoughts seemed to lurch, to show her somewhere that could not possibly be here, for it was untouched by the ravages of war.

A memory, she realized, and yet Kayden was in it.

It was Kayden's arms around her, holding her close to him, Kayden's face leaning closer, filling her vision until her eyes slid closed, and then it was Kayden's lips on her own, his mouth, his kiss, and yet for all that it was his, it was hers too, for she wanted it as he did, wanted him as he wanted her.

Beneath a sky that was nothing like the she one was currently beneath, in a place she instinctively knew to be far from the one she was currently in, she and Kayden held to one another and their kiss was drenched in passion and love and wanting.

Mya stopped trying to work out where or when it had been and she simply gave herself up to the memory. To Kayden, to the feel, the taste, of his mouth as it claimed hers. She relived the kiss and she did not know how she could have forgotten anything that felt so good, so right. She relived it, and she treasured it, and she held it bright and perfect in her memory.

In France she was barely conscious, she stumbled down a war-torn street, walking on the ruins of buildings. But in her mind, she was far from France. In her mind, she remembered kissing. Not a dream. Not distant or foggy, but sharp and clear. Certain as the road in front of her feet.

She remembered kissing Kayden.

Chapter 9

Mya woke with a start. She sat up and looked around, taking a moment to try to orientate herself. She was in her room, dressed in the clothes she'd worn to go outside, and she'd been sleeping on her bed rather than in it. Well, that made sense so far. Her memories of coming back to the hospital were dim and disjointed, but no more than was to be expected, she supposed.

It wasn't home. She knew that much.

It was France. In the convent. In the room she shared with Kayden.

She made a mental note to find and thank the two men who had brought her back, not to mention the long-suffering doctor who had patched her up and sent her to bed to rest for a second time now.

She felt guilty about that. He was busy enough without having to look after her on top of his other duties. Maybe there would be something she could do to help. She didn't think she had any sort of medical knowledge or experience, but she was sure there were things she could find to do to make herself useful around the place. Especially if her memory didn't return any time soon and she found herself staying here for a while. She wasn't quite ready to think about that too deeply just yet, though.

Kayden.

Her eyes jumped to his bed.

It was unoccupied, and she felt an uneasy prickle of worry creep across her skin. She remembered the shell landing, the unbelievable devastation it had caused. She had told her two rescuers that she hadn't seen him since and they had promised her that they would go and look for him. She would, she supposed, have to be content with that.

She was reaching out with her toes to slip one and then the other of her shoes on, rather than braving the stone floor with her bare feet, when a strand of her hair fell in front of her face as she leaned forwards. She looked at it in something akin to horror. Her red hair, of which she was secretly rather proud of, was absolutely filthy. Dull with dust and soot, it hung lank and limp around her face. She'd washed her hands and her face, but she was sure she still looked a fright, and for a moment she was glad that Kayden wasn't there to see, but that led her to worrying for him again.

She stood up carefully, cautiously, ready to sit down again if she felt dizzy, but was actually surprisingly steady. Encouraged she moved to crouch at the end of her bed, and, lifting the lid on the little broken trunk, she looked in at the small selection of mismatched and second-hand clothes it held, which, along with the boots that sat in a tidy pair tucked just beneath the bed, was currently the sum total of her worldly goods. Strangely, the thought heartened her, and she found herself smiling. Small as it was, it was more than she had possessed just days before when Kayden had found her, and it represented the kindness of those she had met since.

It wasn't as though she would be requiring finery any time soon, she told herself, the smile still curving her lips. Her social calendar was as empty as her wardrobe. She reached into the trunk and drew out one of the two pairs of army issue pants she had been given, one a motley of greens and browns. The other, the pair she now held, was black. They were both loose-fitting around her long legs, with more pockets than she could imagine anyone ever needing. They had adjusted to her waist by means of a drawstring, and they closed with a zipper and a large button at the waistband. The belt, which someone had made extra holes in for her with a pocketknife, was rolled into a neat coil beside them, and she fished that out, too, and then the button-down shirt which was black and made from a thick, hard-wearing cotton. Glamorous it was not, she thought, as she finished her selection by grabbing a pair of thick socks and plain black underwear, and then bundled the lot up inside a large towel. It left her trunk almost empty, but she was still smiling as she replaced its battered lid.

She slipped quietly out of her room and began to make her way towards the bathrooms.

Kayden had warned her, in the time they'd had after they had eaten, that the showers often did not run warm for a full cycle. He'd laughed as he'd told the story of his own first experience with one of them, which had gone from a reasonable temperature to frigid halfway through, leaving him scrambling to finish his shower. Mya approached the stall with trepidation, half expecting ice cold water to come shooting out of the shower head.

She need not have worried.

Apparently, the lateness of the hour meant that the convent appeared to be deserted. Everyone who would have bathed was in bed. The corridors and hallways were silent and empty as she moved along them, and when she reached the bathrooms it had been long enough since they were used that the tile on the floor had had time to dry.

She hoped that meant that the water in the tank had time to heat.

It seemed as though it had, because the water was warm from the start through to the very end. Mya took full advantage of the situation, washing her hair twice, rinsing it through for a little longer than it needed and luxuriating in the simple pleasures of the shower, in the little rituals of cleaning and cleansing, and the feeling of warm water cascading over her skin. Despite her self-indulgence the water was still coming out warm when she finally shut it back off. Hoping that her extravagance hadn't cost anyone the same enjoyment, she stepped out onto a simple wooden stand, its flat rungs keeping her feet from the cold tile below, and there she discovered that the steam from the shower had warmed the air of the small cubicle. The little luxury added to her mood, and as she wrapped herself in the towel she felt an absence of the tension that had been building in her, tension she had not even realized she had been carrying with her until she discovered that it was gone.

Mya closed her eyes, relaxing further. Her thoughts, unsurprisingly enough, took her to Kayden. What she found more surprising was that they also took her back to the encounter with the stag, as though thinking of one summoned the other. With distance the incident had taken on a dreamlike quality. It had become a surreal, almost otherworldly happening.

The logical explanation was that the fighting had startled him from his usual forests and fields, had sent him fleeing through the damaged streets of a city, and there she had happened upon him, or he upon her. Yet Mya was sure that their meeting was no mere coincidence, nor was it meaningless. It was something other, something more, and it had significance. It was a significance that she did not yet understand, but just because she didn't know its meaning that did not mean that it did not have one. There were many things that she didn't know the meaning to, after all, yet if they meant nothing then the world would be nothing more than the sum of her knowledge.

Mya smiled.

The words triggered another almost-memory, a woman, a friend, teasing Mya gently about being the center of the universe. Eleanora, she thought. But, as it had been with the memory of the rhyme, so it was with this one, too, and she could not catch hold of it, nor could she expand upon the recollection. So close, yet just out of reach. At least, she told herself, this was consistent with the earlier memory, and she wondered about the two women. Were they her sisters? Her friends? She thought friend more likely, but it made her wonder. Did she, somewhere, have a family who were worried for her? Perhaps even looking for her? She sighed softly. So many questions and so few answers.

She unwound the towel from her body and used it to dry her hair, slowly and methodically, letting the familiar action sooth her. No matter how she tried to push it away she could not help but be worried for Kayden. The thought that something had happened to him, that he could be hurt and alone in the night? It was terrible. Almost too terrible to contemplate. The thought that she could lose him was bad enough, but for it to happen before, before... But there her thoughts trailed off, became as hard to grasp as her memories. Before what? Again she had no answers.

If the stag had become dreamlike to her mind, the kiss, the one that she had been trying to rationalize away by denouncing it as dream, felt to be anything but. She recalled it in a startling clarity that, she knew, her dreams simply did not contain. Yet it made no sense. How could they have met before, and, if they had, how could Kayden not remember? His memory was not the one that contained nothing but gaps. Like a broken tooth it nagged at her sense of rightness, and, like a broken tooth she prodded and pressed at it, yet no answers were forthcoming. The question and the situation both were impossible. How could something be, that could not be? But the knowledge that it was impossible made it no less real. Made her no less sure that it had happened somehow, that in some faraway place she and Kayden had kissed, and that somehow, she remembered it, when she could remember nothing else. The rest of her past might be a sea of uncertainty, but that kiss she was sure of.

Oh, it was frustrating, more so because she was sure that she knew all the answers that were not coming to her. That she held them, in some locked chamber of her mind, and if she could but find the key then all the confusion would be resolved, would fall into place. Mya sighed. This was getting her nowhere. The tension of before was coming back, and she made the effort to relax her shoulders.

She shook out her damp hair and wished, not for the first time, that she had a hairbrush at her disposal. Still, at least the long strands were once more their usual bright auburn color, and she ran her fingers through them, teasing out the tangles, doing the best she could to put her hair to rights.

She dressed, then, buttoning the thick shirt closed, leaving the top two buttons undone, her throat and the line of her collar bones exposed. She tucked the shirt into the pants and threaded the belt through the loops, fastening it around her narrow waist. What would Kayden think, she wondered, smiling. She very much doubted that he would find the outfit to be anything other than ridiculous. She pulled the thick socks on and then laced the boots to her feet. They felt heavy, but were a surprisingly good fit, and if she was honest, they were far more practical than her shoes, far more suited to negotiating the rubble outside.

The dark clothes made her skin seem to be even paler than usual, they brought out the flame bright color of her hair. When she leaned forwards to pick up her dress she caught a glimpse of her reflection in the mirror, and she almost did not recognize herself. The army clothes did not look as odd as she had feared they might. The high waistline of the pants showed off her long legs, and the swell of her hips filled them enticingly. The thick belt accentuated her narrow waist. She had worried that the lack of a bra would be either unflattering or unseemly, but the hint of cleavage that showed above the buttons was neither of those things and when she looked critically at the shirt she decided that its chest pockets and the thick cotton material made it impossible to tell that she was naked beneath it.

Who would have thought that she would be so suited to the army look?

She picked up her dress and discarded underwear and went to the sink, washing them by hand with the soap she had used on her body. They were filthy with soot and grime and it took her some time to get it all out of them, but she persevered, and eventually the water ran clear. As she worked her thoughts went once more to Kayden. If she hadn't been so worried she might have been irritated at how much time she seemed to spend contemplating him. But the worry drowned out all else, and she decided that when she was done here she would find the two men who had promised her that they would go and look for him, and see if they had been successful.

Twenty minutes later she had left her dress hanging to drip dry at one side of the bathroom and she was doing just that, prowling quietly through the equally quiet hallway that led past the wards and down to the two areas that were currently being used as a recreational lounge and a dining area. The mess hall. She grinned at that, imaging Kayden raising his eyebrows at her joking at the term and then laughing at the look on his face. The army seemed to have the strangest terms for everything, but she supposed that anywhere hungry soldiers wolfed down their rations was probably aptly named a mess. She could picture Kayden laughing at her thoughts. That warm deep bass laugh of his that reminded her of sunny days and inexplicably made her feel safe.

However, the recreation lounge was empty when she got there, the radio silent, and only the smell of cigarette smoke still hanging in the air gave any sign of its recent use. Where was Kayden?

The mess hall too was neither messy nor occupied. The long tables had been wiped down and left clean, ready for breakfast, and at the side of the room an urn kept water hot for any late night stragglers, like herself, Mya thought. The enamel mugs and metal pots for the tea were upside down and set out in tidy rows on a drying rack, the sugar in a large glass mason jar and the tea leaves in a tin. She took a tray from the pile and set out a tea-pot, spooning tea leaves into it, and, when she couldn't find a pot to put the sugar into she added it directly to the mixture as she had seen the soldiers do. She preferred her own tea black, but an impulse made her reach for a small jar and pour some milk into it, setting it and two of the mugs onto the tray, just in case Kayden had returned to their room while she had been away. Lastly she filled the pot with water from the urn and then she lifted the tray and made her way back to her room.

It was only as she was leaving that she thought to glance at the clock. Three-thirty in the morning. She must have slept for longer than she had thought. Well, at least that explained why the large building seemed deserted, but, she realized with a sinking heart, it meant that Kayden was unlikely to return. Although, since she had come, they had not been apart at night. He had explained to her that he would soon need to bunk with his unit. She hoped that was where he was now. Safe and out of harm's way. That he was tucked up securely somewhere on the other side of the city, warm and safe and unharmed.

Still, as she hurried back to their room she held onto the hope that he would be there waiting, or perhaps asleep already, that he would laugh at her fears and set them to rest.

He was not.

The room was as empty as it had been when she left it. With a sigh, she set the tray down on the table next to her bed, feeling foolish now for bringing the extra mug and the milk. Then, telling herself firmly that he was fine, she turned back her bed covers and kicked her boots off, put them and her shoes tidily beneath the bed and began to get ready for sleep.

A few minutes later her army pants and socks were folded tidily on the end of her bed and she was sitting in it, still wearing the shirt and panties, her legs stretched out beneath the covers, sipping tea from the enamel mug.

Sleep wouldn't come, however. Her tea finished, she had laid down, turned the little bedside lamp off, and tried to clear her mind, but the silence that settled over the room was loud and lonely, and she caught herself listening for Kayden's breathing, or straining her ears for the sound of the door at the end of the hallway opening, for his quiet footfalls outside. Minutes passed slowly and when, somewhere outside she heard a single clock chiming the hour, and she counted four bells, she put the light back on and sat up.

There was still tea in the pot, but she left it alone and instead she slid out of her bed and went over to the one that Kayden had slept in. She reached out and ran her hands over the still rumpled covers, smiling slightly. He made his bed with a strange precision that spoke to her of OCD but she suspected was more due to his military training. One of his hairs, dark and shining, was on the pillow and she picked it up, wound it absently around her finger, and then she lay down, curling onto the crumpled blankets and burying her face in his pillow, breathing in deeply, inhaling the scent of him. She pulled the covers back and slipped into the bed, pressing herself to the mattress, fitting her body to the slight indentations there, as though by filling the places that he had filled, she could somehow be closer to him.

Beneath the covers his scent was barely detectable. He had apparently slept in his clothes, ready to leap into action without having to delay to dress, but she looped her arms around the pillow, and hugged it, burying her face in it once more, and suddenly her throat was tight and her eyes were burning and she was fighting not to cry. She blinked the tears away and closed her eyes, and imagined that he was here, that she was lying against his chest with his arms protectively around her. It was a soothing thought, and she held onto it as she could not hold onto her elusive memories, cuddling it to her as she cuddled his pillow, and it carried her down into sleep.

Chapter 10

Mya woke to early morning sunlight spilling across her face, and an empty room. Kayden still had not returned. Outside, she saw no sign of soldiers moving through the rubble, though there were people here and there, civilians, likely searching for some piece of their lives that had not been destroyed in the bombing. Worry made a tight knot in the pit of Mya's stomach.

What if Kayden had been hurt? Should she search the other rooms of the hospital for him? The second cup of tea still sat on the tray she'd brought in from the mess hall, cold and untouched.

The nurses would know, surely, if something had happened to Kayden. Or would he had been taken somewhere else? What if he was too badly injured to be returned here? Mya tried not to let those thoughts linger, pushing them out of her head as she dressed herself in the pants and button-up, pulled on her boots and tied them. Wherever Kayden was, he was well. He must be. She would know if he were injured, would she not? Would know if something had happened to him. She was certain she would feel it in her bones.

So he must be well. She simply had to find some means of occupying her time until he returned.

The bump on her head was still tender, Mya discovered as she worked her fingers through her hair, coaxing out the knots that had tied themselves in the night so she could braid it back. But her head no longer ached. She supposed that was something to be grateful for.

Dressed in the clothes she had worn the previous night, and as presentable as she could be, she made her way out into the hall and began yet again with her search for Kayden. It was as fruitless as the one the night before had been. There was no sign of him, and even when she worked up the courage to ask one or two of the friendlier looking men if they had seen him, they could not recall when they'd spoken with him last. Mya tried not to let that worry her, though the knot in her stomach had tightened.

She thought about returning to the room that they shared. Kayden must come back eventually, surely? She should be there to greet him when he did. But what if he did not return immediately? She could hardly remain in the room forever, waiting for him to come back. She sighed. Dithering around was pointless. It was hardly going to help the situation, and besides, she did not think she was the sort of woman who dithered. She had just decided to go and check the wards, perhaps ask the nuns if anyone had been brought in during the night, when she turned a corner in the corridor and found herself face to face with the doctor. She smiled warmly at him, rather relieved to find a familiar face.

"Ah, Mademoiselle Boyle." He returned her smile, rearranging the clipboard and folders that he held against his chest so that he could offer her his hand. "I was wondering when I would see you."

Mya, momentarily confused, took the offered hand and returned his shake, the gesture an automatic reflex while she wondered at his remark. Then, with a slightly guilty start she remembered that she had promised him the night before that she would return this morning so that he could check her over. Worry for Kayden had put it completely from her mind.

"And here I am." She answered brightly, deciding not to mention that she had forgotten their appointment, and hoping that she had done nothing to give it away.

"*Oui.* Yes, you are," he agreed amicably enough. If he had noticed he gave no sign, and instead, gesturing for her to accompany him, he led them, rather briskly, to the room she had been brought to the previous night. She followed him in, taking in details that she had been in no fit state to make sense of during that last visit. He must, she realized as she looked around, be using it for some sort of consultation room, probably for those, like herself, whose injuries were not serious enough that they needed to be admitted to one of the wards. The walking wounded; the expression had seemed to float to the surface of her mind and Mya wondered if it were the correct one, but the doctor was reading from his clipboard, his expression intent, and she didn't want to interrupt him with what felt like such an unimportant question. Especially if the answer was wrong. She had no wish to seem a fool in his eyes.

"*Une minute, s'il vous plait.*" He placed the folders on the table and pulled the chair that was tucked beneath it out without looking up from the clip-board, gesturing to the other one with his free hand in a slightly distracted manner.

"Thank you." Mya answered, but he nodded and continued to read and so she resumed her silent perusal of the room. The cluttered table that was presumably serving as his desk was strewn with papers and small stacks of precariously balanced manila folders, pens were dotted at irregular intervals in the small spaces between them, and a sealed plastic box that may have been a first aid kit sat half on and half off one of its edges. The table was pushed tight against the wall, and a bunk which Mya remembered lying on the previous night ran the length of the wall opposite. The wall at the far end of the room held the window and a chart with various sized letters that became smaller from top to bottom. Mya knew without knowing how she knew, that it was for testing eyesight. A neat row of boxes stacked two high ran along the bottom of every bit of wall clear of furniture and to Mya's inexperienced eye they appeared to contain an array of things such as bandages and dressings, small plastic measuring cups sealed individually into see-through bags, thin latex gloves. There were two mismatched chairs, too, the one the doctor in the room were mismatched. One was a plastic armless thing with metal legs, such as one might find in a school. It looked less comfortable than sitting on the floor would have been, Mya thought. Luckily for Mya she would not have to find out, for that was the one he was settling into, the other was also armless with metal legs but at least it had padding.

"And how are you feeling today?"

"Better," she told him. "And please, call me Mya." She smiled. "I think you have patched me up enough that we are past formalities."

"As you wish." His answer sounded a little awkward, and Mya was suddenly worried that she had offended him.

"By first name terms, I mean, of course," she said quickly, "that you call me Mya and I call you Doctor."

He smiled. "My name is Jean-Luc, but you may call me doctor if you wish." He turned in his chair and went through the folders on the table, finding the one he sought and pulling it carefully from a pile. The others tottered warningly, but somehow managed to avoid sliding en masse to the floor.

The doctor glanced down at the file in his hand and huffed, tossing it back on top of the pile. Evidently it wasn't the one that he was looking for.

"So," he said as he slid files aside in an attempt to find hers, which, Mya thought with a little bit of amusement, he would have placed in the stack less than two days before. "While you are here, you might tell me how Lieutenant McGregor is doing. He has not damaged himself any further, I hope?"

Mya bit her lip. "Actually," she said. "I was hoping that you might be able to help me with that. He ran out last night, when that shell went off, and I haven't seen him since."

She tried to keep the nervous worry out of her voice, not sure what the doctor would think of someone being so concerned for a man they hardly knew, but he was too absorbed in going through files to notice anything out of place in her voice.

"If he'd come through here, I would have seen him, no? But we can watch for him, if you wish. I will alert you if he is brought in."

That was both a relief and a new worry. Kayden wouldn't have been brought to the doctor if he hadn't been hurt, but what if he hadn't ever even made it out of the field?

"I would appreciate that," she said, because asking the doctor about Kayden's chances of survival wasn't likely to be at all comforting. "Thank you."

She watched him scramble to catch a stack of files that had given up at last on its position and started sliding over the rest of them toward the floor.

"Actually, I might be able to help you with something."

He looked up, and the expression on his face was weary resignation. Obviously he had been dealing with the folder stacks for long enough to know that he would eventually lose his fight to keep them on the table and in their proper stacks.

"And what is that?"

Mya nodded toward the paperwork that was currently trying to make a break for it. "I could take care of that for you. Help you around the hospital, if you like. Fetch and carry. Any minor cleaning duties. Paperwork."

He hardly even took a moment to consider it before he was nodding. "I believe something of that nature could be arranged."

And it would give her a chance to check the men coming in, and see if one of them was Kayden. Her stomach twisted nervously at the thought, but it was better to know than to sit in her room and worry over something she couldn't do anything about.

"Ah-hah!" The doctor emerged from the pile of folders triumphant, a file held in one hand, and carefully shoved the others back into place before the stacks dismantled themselves. "Here we are, no?"

Sitting up a little straighter in her seat, Mya leaned forward to get a glimpse of the file. It was just a handwritten page, done in a rapid scribble that was probably hard to read on the best of days.

"I'll have to trust your judgment on that."

He glanced down at the file in his hand, making a thoughtful sound. "Head injury?"

"Yes," Mya said. "I'm not quite sure how I got it, but you knew that already, I think."

"Yes, yes. That one." His brow furrowed. "You are still having trouble with your memory?"

"Unfortunately." Mya sighed, and settled back a little in the chair as the doctor opened the file and scanned through its single page of data, sinking down to sit.

"Any other symptoms? Dizziness? Nausea?"

Mya shook her head. "Not that I've noticed. I've had a few strange dreams, but I think that's about the extent of it."

That got him interested. He leaned forward in his seat. "What sort of dreams?"

"Very vivid ones," Mya said. "The sort that feel as though I'm living a memory rather than simply having a dream."

"And what sort of memories are you living?"

Mya's eyebrows lifted above the smile she gave him. "You're doing an entirely different type of head check than I expected, Doctor."

He shook his head. "It would seem that way, perhaps. But knowing what memories come to you will tell me something of what kind of injury you might have."

"I dream about Kayden," Mya admitted. "But not the Kayden I met here." She took a deep breath and let it out again slowly through her nose. The doctor's eyes were on her, intent and listening. He said nothing, and Mya went on. "I dream of him somewhere else. In... Before this war. Before I ever came to France. And yet he says he does not remember me."

She looked down at her hands, twisting together in her lap. It was a strange thing to have to explain to a doctor. It was a strange thing to explain to anyone. She had, at the last minute, backed out of saying she believed the memories came from another era entirely. That she might have known him before the war, before either of them left Scotland, was not entirely impossible. Indeed, it was not even implausible. The highlands were not particularly dense in their population, and it was from them that both she and Kayden had come. The notion that she had dreamed of something beyond that was more than she was willing to admit to. More than she was sure she believed herself. Dreams were strange things, and she would have put it down to that, had they not seemed so concrete. So embedded in a past she could not remember.

"Perhaps," the doctor suggested, "It is not Kayden that you dream of, but someone you knew once. Maybe your mind, in replacing your missing memories, chose a face you recognized in your altered state. The process of adjusting to amnesia can be a difficult one, and strange. It is doing the best it might with the information it has."

It was a reasonable explanation. Perfectly logical, in fact. But it struck Mya as wrong. She could not imagine even subconsciously allowing another, however dear to her, to wear Kayden's face. Did not think she would carve a place in her memories for a person that was not the person they seemed.

"Maybe," she said, and offered nothing more.

There was a moment of silence between them, short and awkward, before the doctor spoke again.

"It's a good sign that you're no longer sick, and that your head does not ache. Despite the lack of memory, I believe you are healed enough to be up and about. Though I caution you. If you do become ill, see that you rest. It will do you no good to push on and harm yourself further."

"I'll be careful about it," Mya said. "And step out if I need to."

"Then I see no reason why you should not be allowed to help here." He smiled a little ruefully. "As you can see, there is something of a mess in my office."

The mess was hard to miss. Mya dipped her head to hide her own smile, straightened out her expression. When she nodded, she was serious. "I'd be happy to help you organize it. I know that it must not be an easy job, running a military hospital like this."

"I will speak also with the nuns," he said, rising from the uncomfortable-looking chair he'd been sitting in. "And ask them if there is anything you might do to help in their care of the wounded. I am sure they would not turn down an offer."

That would be a chance to make certain that Kayden hadn't showed up in the hospital. "I would appreciate that," Mya said.

"Then, if you wish, you may start now here, and I will speak to them while I am out checking up on patients."

He gave her a quick, polite nod, and hurried out of the room. Mya sat for a moment, considering the stacks of paperwork on every flat surface, and sighed. She hadn't signed herself up for an easy job, but neither had anyone else at the convent. If they could go on, day after day, doing what they did, then she could handle a little paperwork.

Chapter 11

A full day now, and Kayden still had not returned. Mya had gone through the doctor's piles of paper, setting them up in categories rated most urgent to least. There were still stacks of files on his desk, but at least they were no longer haphazard and threatening to topple over at the slightest provocation. The doctor had been rather grateful for the change.

The nuns seemed equally pleased to have her among their number. They were not talkative women, for the most part, but they were kind, and Mya had more than once found herself watching silently as one tended to a patient, admiring the iron strength beneath the soft exterior. She herself mostly ran errands, though she did once or twice aid in some of the less complicated medical procedures. There were only two qualified nurses, and they were assigned the hardest cases. Mya didn't envy them their duties. There had been no sign of Kayden among the wounded.

She was carrying a stack of files bound for the doctor's desk when she nearly ran directly into one of the men who had helped her return to the convent two nights before.

"Pardon me, mademoiselle," he said instantly, taking a step back out of her path and looking apologetic as she scrambled to keep the papers from falling out of her arms.

"Oh," Mya said. "It's no trouble. I ought to have been watching where I was going. I-" She paused, looking up at the familiar face and trying to remember where she had seen him before. Then it hit her. "You were one of the men who helped me before. When the shell fell. I don't think I ever learned your name."

He smiled. "It is Henri. I am glad to see that you are well, though it looks that the doctor is working you to your bones."

Mya laughed. "He's getting his money's worth. Or would be. If he was paying me." She held the files a little closer to her chest, as though they could guard her against bad news, against an answer she didn't want to hear to the question she was about to ask. "You wouldn't happen to know what happened to Kayden, would you?"

"I am sorry. I would not." His expression was once more an apology. Then he brightened. "Though I am to be out today. I might check for you, where he bunks."

"Could you?" Mya felt a rush of gratitude at the offer. "I would not want to be any kind of trouble, but if it's on your way and you could see whether he's injured or not, I would be so grateful."

Henri chuckled. "It is no trouble, mademoiselle. I do not mind helping you keep an eye on the man of your dreams." He winked at her with the words, and Mya felt her cheeks heat. She hadn't thought her feelings for Kayden were quite so obvious. "I will drop by the camp where his regiment stays and see if they are perhaps about."

"Thank you," Mya said, because she wasn't sure what else to say. She didn't know how to respond to the statement that Kayden was the man of her dreams. It was true enough in its way, but she hadn't exactly gone about shouting that to the rooftops, and she would prefer that it didn't spread through the makeshift hospital.

"I will return in the evening, and let you know," he said, and then he was on his way again, and Mya was continuing down toward the doctor's office with her stack of files.

She wondered what he had discovered as she ran the rest of her errands - carrying bowls of water out to the doctor or fetching a roll of bandages, occasionally pausing to chat with a wounded soldier here or there. She made sure to smile at them, hoping that the simple gesture might at least brighten their days. It was little enough to do.

In a spare moment, she remembered the door that she and Kayden had run through, and fetched oil to grease the hinges so they would not squeak so the next time it was opened.

In the early afternoon, they brought in a man who had been too close to one of the bombs when it dropped. Mya watched them carrying him in on the stretcher, her heart for a moment jumping into her throat when she spotted dark hair and broad shoulders, but it was not Kayden. This man was smaller. Not nearly so handsome. Which, Mya thought guiltily, was not something she ought to be thinking about a man who had just lost his leg to a German bomb. Her stomach twisted.

He wasn't making much noise, apparently already dosed with what little pain medication they could afford and drifting on the cloud of it. The nuns hurried to his side as he was settled down in a bed, and Mya wondered whether she ought to join them. She wasn't sure she could bring herself to go any closer. Her eyes kept wanting to see Kayden there, wounded and bleeding, his eyes rolled back and his head lolling on the stretcher. A little change of fortune, and it could have been him there in that moment, and she would not have known until they brought him in. She forced herself to look away, and tried to think of other things.

By the time Henri arrived, she was desperate for news. When she saw him in the hall, she hurried to his side. He saw her coming, and his expression tightened. It wasn't the sign she had hoped for. Her stomach lurched. What had happened?

"Henri?" She tried to keep the fear from her voice. "Did you find anything?"

"He is not hurt, so far as I know," Henri said. "And that is the good news, yes? But I am afraid that he and his regiment have left."

Left. Mya stopped in her tracks, slumping back against the cool stone of the wall. Kayden wasn't injured, but Kayden was gone. Left without a word to her.

"For where?"

Henri lifted one shoulder in a shrug and let it fall again. "That I cannot say. Their bunks were empty when I arrived, everything packed up and taken with them."

"They're coming back, though."

The Frenchman shook his head. "I cannot say." He hesitated. "There was no sign they planned a return. I am sorry, mademoiselle."

No sign they planned a return.

He hadn't said a word about it. But then, when would he have had time? The rational part of Mya knew that if Kayden had been called away suddenly, it wasn't his fault that he hadn't had time to tell her that he was leaving. And in truth, he hardly knew her. They had shared a room for all of one night. He was hardly beholden to her.

But the part of her that knew him from dreams, that lit up in his presence and longed for his touch, could not understand why he had not at least bothered to send a note. Her Kayden would have, she was sure.

Her Kayden. He could very well be nothing but a figment of her imagination. The result of a too-hard blow to the head.

"Bad day?"

It took May a moment to realize the question was directed at her. She lifted her eyes, had to tilt her head back to look up at the man who was standing in front of her, regarding her with a sardonic smile.

There was something strangely familiar about him. Something that made Mya's stomach turn.

"Something like that," She said, moving to brush past the red-haired man blocking her way.

"There are better options than Kayden McGregor."

Mya went still. "I suppose," she said slowly, "That you're offering yourself up as an alternative?"

He smiled and held out a hand like he wanted to shake hers. "A superior one. I'm Lachlan. And trust me, I'll make you forget all about him."

"As generous as that is," Mya said, pressing forward and ignoring the offered hand. She didn't want to touch him any more than she had to. "I think I'll pass."

She could feel his glare on her back as she walked away.

Chapter 12

Kayden walked quietly through the corridors of the quiet convent. He was exhausted, and the injury on his side where the bullet had grazed him throbbed painfully. The new bruises and grazes he'd collected ached miserably and he suspected he might have cracked a rib, for it hurt like a son of a bitch when he breathed in deeply. *Three days.* He wanted nothing more than a wash and a long sleep. It was so late, everyone sleeping on this end of the building.

So why was he here?

Why had he looked down at the welcome comfort of his bunk and then, at the last moment, changed his mind and walked across the city to come back to the room that almost felt like home?

Because, he admitted to himself, it was not the room that felt like home, but Mya. She had fallen into his life and instantly become part of it. She was like nobody he had ever met and at the same time she was impossibly familiar.

He knew things about her that he could not possibly have known. He knew how she looked, wrapped in nothing but a sheet, half silhouetted against a window, turning back towards him with her lips slightly parted in that smile he adored. He knew the way her hair smelled when it was wet with the rain, and how her sweet breath came warm and soft against his neck as she slept, curled close to him.

And he knew that he could not bear to lose her again.

None of which made the slightest bit of sense. He was a down to earth man, he would have said of himself had he been asked. A believer in the things his eyes told him. He was more inclined to science than to faith, and he certainly was not given to flights of fancy about beautiful fey women who appeared out of nowhere to steal his heart, and apparently, his sanity.

He cautiously pushed the door to the room open, not wishing to wake Mya. He slipped silently inside, turning to close the door as quietly as he had opened it, so it was not until he'd taken a step toward his bed that he realized it was occupied. He froze, momentarily at a complete loss as to what to do.

In that moment Mya opened those startlingly green eyes of hers and smiled sleepily up at him. He was hit with a sense of Deja vu, of having been here and done this before, somewhere else, in some other time.

"Kayden," Mya said, her voice slurred with sleep, and then she startled fully awake, eyes wide, realizing that she was still in his bed, but probably more importantly, that he was here, and as far as she could tell, he was unharmed. She sat up, running her hands through her hair, pushing it back from her face with little, automatic gestures.

"I'm so glad you're back." She slipped long, bare legs out from under the covers and stood, crossing to his side. "I thought you were gone." She reached for him, her hand going to his face, gentle and tender as it stroked its way across his cheek and then stopped, her fingers resting against his cheekbone, her thumb just beneath the firm line of his jaw. "They told me that you weren't coming back.

Kayden leaned into the touch, his eyebrows drawing together as he looked down at her. "Who told you that?"

"Henri. The man who helped me the night the bomb fell. He went to look for your regiment, and-" She cut herself off, apparently realizing a more pressing concern. "Are you hurt?" Her voice was low, worried. Her other hand was already going to his coat, her fingers quick and clever as one after another she undid the buttons. He opened his eyes slowly and appeared to consider the question, he sensed her heart beating faster, worry in her movements now as she carefully reached up to slip the coat from around his shoulders.

He complied, pulling his arms free and letting the heavy garment slide away to fall in a forgotten heap on the floor. "We were sent out on a reconnaissance mission, but we were always going to come back, Mya."

I would not have left you without at least a farewell.

"Kayden?" she asked again, her tone concerned, "Are you hurt? Shall I get the doctor?"

He shook his head. "No lass, it's nothing. Let him sleep."

"What's nothing?" For a moment her voice was sharp with fear, but it gentled quickly. "Let me see." She reached out again, this time targeting the buttons on his shirt.

He looked her up and down, and despite his tiredness his dark eyes flashed in the low light and his laugh became a wince and then a chuckle. He reached up to his shirt, but her answering expression as she met his eyes said that she didn't share his entertainment, and she pushed his hands away. He let her, let them drop back to his sides.

"I was worried." she said softly. "The shell—there was a shell, and when everything settled you were gone, and I couldn't see you." Her voice shook slightly. "I was so afraid that something terrible had happened."

I was so afraid that I had lost you.

She didn't say it, but he could see the words written across her face, as clearly as though she'd spoken them aloud.

He shook his head. "No, I—" His mind caught up with her words. The laughter fled from him. "You were outside? When that happened?" He gestured towards the window with his hand, the movement taking in the street outside, the new damage.

She nodded, mutely. If she spoke she thought she might cry. In fact, she looked as though she might cry anyway. But if she spoke there would definitely be no stopping the tears she had held in all night.

"Och, Mya." Now it was his voice that was full of concern. "What were you thinking, lass? You could've been hurt. You could've been killed. What made you go out into the street?"

Mya shook her head again. "You did," she whispered quietly. "I don't know. I thought if you were there I should be there, too." But even as she was saying the words she must have realized how strange they sounded, how little sense they made.

He wondered what she was doing following him out into the night. It was dangerous out there.

"I thought," she tried instead, and stumbled over the words. "It came down, and then everything was crazy and I, I thought, I couldn't see you, and I thought you were—" She couldn't bring herself to say it. It was too awful.

He pulled her gently to him. "Mya. Mya." His arms slipped around her and she leaned against him. One of her hands was still between them, fumbling with the buttons on his shirt.

She moved it, flat across his chest, slid it around his side, holding close to him, and he rested his cheek against her hair.

"Don't be getting hurt, lassie." His voice had never sounded so gentle to anyone before, and then he knew, without a doubt, he had spoken to her before like this. Another time. In another place. But he continued, almost a whisper, "I couldn't bear it." Anguish was tangled in his words, and his breath caught.

"Kayden," she whispered back, because there weren't words for what they were feeling, or if there were, they didn't know them. She held tight to him, breathed in the scent of him, warm and faintly musky, overlaid with fresh sweat that had no right to smell as good as it did. "Kayden."

His hands came up to run through her hair, stroking through the thick strands, and then his fingers closed and tugged it gently. She went with the slight pull, tilting her head up as his mouth came down and captured hers, hard and possessive. He wanted to sink into the kiss. He wanted to be closer to her. Feel of her skin against his own. He wanted to be inside of her. *Fuck*, he wanted. He wanted everything at once. Sooner.

Her hands were almost ripping at the buttons of his shirt, and still it was too slow, still there was too much between them. She broke the kiss to peel the shirt from him, and he stepped back just far enough to free his arms, one and then the other. His shirt fell from him, drifting down to join his coat on the floor, forgotten as soon as it left his body, and her hands slid flat over his chest, feeling taut muscle beneath her fingers, his skin warm against her palms.

"Mya." There was an almost anguished note to his voice still, but it was low, husky with wanting, and the fear that had been there was gone, replaced with something else entirely. She looked up, green eyes meeting dark eyes that were darker yet, filled with need, and she knew that he wanted all that she did. His fingers went to the buttons of her shirt as though in confirmation, and one by one they melted open beneath his deft touch.

Their eyes stayed locked together as she changed the direction of her hands, drew them downward, slowly, fingertips that became light nails, dragging lightly across his chest, and the sound that he made began as a sharp intake of breath and turned into a low, throaty moan. The breath tore at his side, creating pain that mixed with pleasure. Another button, and then he had undone her shirt. It melted from her shoulders, baring her breasts and dropping away until the sleeves caught its fall, and it draped into graceful folds behind the small of her back. He dragged his eyes from hers then, and they moved slowly over her, as though imprinting the image forever onto his memory. She looked right back at him, a slight smile on her flushed features, beautiful and proud and not in the least disconcerted by his scrutiny.

"I want you, Kayden McGregor." The words were light, teasing, almost a challenge.

Kayden responded with a smile. He swallowed hard before he answered, and the set of his jaw was at odds with the casual flavor of his words. "I should hope so." This time when his eyes swept down and then back up again the look was pointed, though he made no attempt to conceal that he liked what he saw, want still stark on his features, his eyes hungry. "Because if you didn't," he continued, fingers ghosting over the skin she'd begun stripping him to check for damage. "I'd be reading this situation all wrong, and the advancements in modern medicine aren't at all what I've been led to believe."

Mya couldn't help but laugh. "You make a fine point," she conceded, but she wasn't going to let him get away with making it look quite so easy. She took her hands from his chest and put them behind herself to free her shirt from her arms, drawing her shoulders back, her breasts lifting as the shirt dropped to the floor.

Kayden swallowed again and Mya smiled. "And you a fine figure," he said. The teasing was gone from him and his voice was rough. "You are, Mya. You're the most beautiful thing I've ever seen."

"Several," Mya said, and a rough edge had crept into her own voice, "fine points." And then her hands were on his body again, reaching around his sides and running her nails down his back, leaving thin red stripes to mark where they had been. He pulled her closer, pressing his body to hers, and she went with the pull, feeling her breasts flatten against the warmth of his chest, his arms tighten around her.

One of her hands crept up into his hair, her fingers spreading as they slid into the soft strands, closing again, becoming a fist, tugging gently to pull his head down to her mouth, and claiming a hungry kiss, nipping at his lips and then slipping her tongue between them when they parted.

He met her tongue with his own, and for long moments the kiss gentled, became a thing to be savored, a slow exploration of each other's mouths and a tender entwining of tongues. Mya eyes slid closed and she clung to him, falling into the kiss, the taste of her mouth filling his own. He was solid and real and she was safe and wanted in his arms.

He moaned against her mouth, and, too hungry to keep to a slow pace they let the kiss build. Sharp teeth grazed soft skin, nipped and bruised at tender flesh. Kayden found himself moaning again, long and low, sounding almost a growl, and Mya moaned an answer, the sound muffled against his lips, but wanting, wanton. She drew back slowly and broke the kiss, whispered something that might have begun as his name but came out as two tangled syllables that formed no word but spoke clearly of wanting. Of desire.

Her hand dropped from his hair to flatten against his back, moving together with the one already there, reaching out and gliding over his broad shoulders to feel the sculpted symmetry of the muscles beneath her palms. She read the shape of them with her fingertips as her hands moved slowly downward. They reached the barrier of his belt too soon, and she paused there, traced her fingers along the line of it around his middle, moving slowly, too slowly, emphasizing the path of her hands with light touches of her nails.

Kayden groaned, rolling his hips and pressing himself against her, sinuous and slow. Her hands left the warmth of his flesh behind so they could continue their downward journey, her fingers spreading again as her hands moved over his buttocks, then curling around the curve of them, pulling him to her, and now it was she who writhed, rubbing herself against him, feeling his hard length pressing through the fabric of the combat trousers, straining against it as though eager to escape.

She drew her breath in sharply, let it out in a soft and wanting moan, her fingers drawing him closer. "Is there anywhere that you are not solid muscle?" she whispered and then chuckled softly. "If there is, I haven't yet found it." Her fingers kneaded slightly, and his hips rolled again pressing his length hard against her as she writhed, and oh, but she wanted it. She wanted him. He knew that without a doubt.

His hands had been stroking her back, holding her close but now, as he rolled his hips, matching his movements to hers, one of his hands came up to cup her breast, kneading it, and his hands, for all that they were calloused with work, felt soft and smooth against the satin of her flesh. He hardened it still further as his thumb moved over her nipple, and her moan became a gasp.

"Kay...den," she said, voice faltering over the word as his index finger came to join his thumb, as her nipple was rolled between the two and her back arched, pressed her demandingly into his hand. His touch sent sparks of sensation scattering over her nerve endings, and each pass of his thumb had her moaning, leaning into him.

"Yes, lass?" The torture was as unbearable for him as it appeared to be for her.

"You're wearing too many clothes." She panted and caught her breath. "You're wearing too many clothes and I wanted you." His hand squeezed her breast tighter as she spoke.

He wanted her to take his clothes off, wanted to take her right now. But he couldn't quite remember how to ask, wasn't sure if he even knew the words any more. Did he remember how to even speak?

"Kayden, dammit, Kayden." Her tone was question and demand both, insistent and yearning. She leaned in and bit his neck for good measure, and then she somehow managed to pull back from his hips. Her hands moved into the space she had created between them. One went to his belt, the other wrapped itself around his cock through his trousers, rubbed slowly along his shaft.

His hips bucked and then settle again, he moaned, swore under his breath, low and quiet and urgent. He pressed himself into her hand, but she kept to the same slow pace, her fingers rippling as they stroked him through the thick material, gripping and loosening along his length. He swore again and his hips moved faster, but she moved her hand with them, teasing him, stroking slowly, slowly, but just fast enough.

"Mya." His voice was strangled, broken. His fingers left her nipple, stroked gently, too gently, over her breast, cupping it again, and before she could protest his mouth had taken its place, and she had to lean on him to steady herself as the flood of sensation hit her, as he sucked the hard bud of flesh into his mouth, his teeth grazing and nipping, and his tongue flicking over the tip, sending tingling jolt after jolt sparking through her body.

He moaned, knowing what he was doing to her. She was coming undone, what little control she could cling to crumbling away.

Her free hand worked on his belt, unfastening the buckle and pulling the end free. Kayden's hand came to join it, undid the button at the fly, then the zip, and then her hand released his cock so that he could push the trousers down his legs, kick off his boots and socks and then after what seemed like an eternity he was stepping free of the last of his clothing.

He sensed that she wanted to look at him, but her view was obscured by his head as he bent it to her breast, so he drew slowly back, teeth grazing against sensitive skin and making her moan, his name lost somewhere in the sound.

He stepped back, and it was her turn to run her eyes over him, the sight no less welcome, no less attractive, for being a familiar one.

He had no patience for the mystery at that particular moment, no interest in wondering yet again why everything about her was familiar. Even the feel of her hand on his cock was one he knew intimately. But he couldn't bring himself to care about that just now, he just wanted to become reacquainted with her. With all of her.

Chapter 13

He stood as proud beneath her eyes as she had for his, and little wonder, she thought. He was absolutely gorgeous. The muscle beneath his skin added a definition that she couldn't help but be drawn to, more than drawn to. The sight of him made her heart beat faster, made her stomach clench inside, and sent a warm flush through her, beginning low in her stomach and between her legs and spreading outward, until it infused her entire being.

Kayden let her look, and then he reached out and hooked a finger into the side of her underwear, twisting it into them. The twist bunched them up, pulled them tight against her sex, made her suddenly aware of how wet she was. How hot and ready for him. The fabric tightened further, drawn over her sensitive flesh and she moaned involuntarily, the sound soft and sweet.

Kayden's hold did not loosen as he stepped back, drawing her after him to the bed. She went willingly, letting him lead her the short distance, taking a small step to the very edge of the narrow mattress as he slid backwards onto it, kneeling there, his free hand catching her hip, strong fingers curling around the curve, the point of the bone nestled against his palm, holding her still as he leaned in and put his face to her, breathing in her scent. He lifted his head slightly and kissed her through the material of her panties, nipping gently, making her gasp as his teeth grazed over her labia, touched against her clit.

"Kayden, oh yes, Kayden." She pressed against him, wanting him to do it again, wanting more, but he pressed back, open mouthed, and breathed slowly out, his breath hot against her heat. "Kayden..." She moaned gently, torn. Half of her wanted to savor the feeling, to draw it out and make it last, possibly forever. But the other half didn't want to wait a moment longer. Then his teeth were moving over her again, tiny little bites that had her hips hitching in erratic jerks, her hands reaching down to slide into his hair.

"Want you," she managed to say, her hands tugging gently, rubbing herself against his mouth as it nipped and teased, and she realized that he knew her body as well as she knew his, knew exactly where to bite, exactly where to place his teeth so that he could catch her clit carefully between them, knew exactly how much pressure she liked. This was not the exploratory touch of a new lover. It was too precise and right and perfect. She moaned again and swore beneath her breath as he licked her, his tongue hot through the fabric that covered her. The sensation chased her thoughts away, leaving no room for anything else.

He was sliding her panties down her legs then, letting them fall to her ankles, his hands going back to her hips. She stepped out of them, lifted one of her feet and rested it on the edge of the bed, bending her knee and letting it drop so that her thighs parted, spreading her open, and it was his turn to swear, low and quiet and fervent as he looked at her, as those dark eyes took in the sight displayed for them. He leaned forwards as though drawn, and his mouth went to the soft folds between her thighs, sucking them gently, and then less gently, working his way around her hidden entrance, his tongue swiping across it and tasting her, then following that taste deeper.

Mya's hands tightened in his hair and she pressed down to meet his tongue as it probed deeper. It wasn't enough. It wasn't enough and he knew it. He was teasing her on purpose. She tugged sharply on his hair and he pulled out, dragged his tongue up the length of her to her clit. It teased there, too, licking just that little bit too gently. Again she knew he was doing it on purpose, and again it struck her that he knew her too well for this to be their first time, how hard was just right, how hard was not quite enough. Holding his head still with his hair she pressed against him, rocking herself against his mouth, and that too was something she would not have done with a stranger, with a first time lover, but she knew, like she knew so much else about him, that he liked her to do so.

If she had needed confirmation, it was there in his low moan, in the tiny kisses he managed to press to her as she writhed against him. He slid a finger into her, one became two. They pressed inside and spread slightly, they moved together and then slid to and fro against one another. And it was good. It was good in a way that only someone intimately acquainted with her body could make it. His fingers danced inside her, they curled forwards until they found the perfect spot, just there and they rubbed hard little circles, one way and then the other, pulling moans that were almost sobs from her. His tongue moved against her clit, swiping over it and leaving her gasping. She was close, and every long lick of his tongue or stroke of his clever fingers took her closer.

"Kayden," there was a cautionary note to her voice as she said his name. A slight stutter as waves of sensation swept through her body, as she felt the orgasm build and crest, and then her hands formed fists, holding his hair tightly in her fingers, her thighs shuddered and tightened, and she was coming, hard and overwhelming, sweeping her away in a rush of feeling and emotion. She cried out, utterly oblivious to any who might be sleeping in the rooms nearby, utterly oblivious to everything that wasn't Kayden, Kayden. His hands, his tongue, him. Kayden.

He slowed, stopped before her heightened senses made her too sensitive, slipped his fingers carefully from her, and with one last, strangely tender kiss to her clit he reached up and pulled her down, boneless and still breathing hard, to the bed with him, he wrapped his arms around her and his mouth sought hers. And when they kissed, long and gentle and passionate, he held her to him as though she was something breakable, something infinitely precious. And his.

The stillness could not last. He was too hungry for her, hard against her hip, and he could not help but move against her. She smiled and reached up to stroke his face, her fingers tracing the outline of his jaw, the planes of his cheek, the line of the bone. She let her own want build again, and as he writhed against her she crawled a little higher up his body and straddled his hips. Lowering herself until the touched, until the warm wetness between her thighs met his hard length and she drew herself along it, felt the head, the ridge behind, slide between her labia, and rub against her clit.

He moved as though he had forgotten how to keep still, all but bucking beneath her, and her long lashes met as her eyes fell shut and she continued to slide along his shaft, rubbing herself against him, and she was certain that this too was something they had done together, taken further, but that was not what she had in mind for this night. Instead she reached down, between her thighs, and wrapped her hand around his cock, her fingers sliding in the wetness she had left upon its flesh. She rubbed her hand along the shaft, rippled her fingers against the slippery slickness, let them glide over the smooth skin, spreading the evidence of his desire along his whole length, and then she lifted him, and when she rocked backwards, and took him inside her, they fitted perfectly, felt just as she had known they would, two parts of a puzzle reunited.

Mya continued to rock her hips, first just the head, and then taking him a little deeper, a little further, with each slow slide until eventually he had hilted within her. He looked up at her, his dark eyes full of emotion, and when he said her name his voice was raw. He reached up to rest his hands on her hips, and then he began to move beneath her. His hips rolled and he thrust upwards, gently at first, his thrusts meeting her movements, matching her pace.

They moved together to a rhythm she knew as intimately as she knew the beat of his heart beneath her hand.

She knew, too, the way that his body tensed as he approached orgasm. The way that his hands tightened around her hips. Mya picked up her pace, driving them both toward the edge that waited, their gasps and moans breaking the quiet of the room.

"Mya," Kayden groaned, voice low and rough at its edges, the word sliding into a sound that was not speech.

"Yes," Mya said, and didn't know what she was saying yes too, just knew that she wanted it. Wanted him. Everything that he would give her.

His eyes were half-lidded, dazed and dark with pleasure. She looked down into them, losing herself in the depths. Kayden filled her senses, the room fading away around them. She let her head drop forward, her hair falling down around them so that the ends of the long strands brushed against his skin with every rise of his chest, every slide of her body against his own.

He growled. Close. She knew it. Could feel it under her own skin, promising to spark into flame with just a little more. One more thrust. His blunt nails digging into her skin. His body shuddering under her own. Mya gasped and came, his name a wreck of syllables on her tongue as pleasure burst through her in a wash of heat, like light filling her up from the inside.

She felt Kayden's hips stutter. His rhythm faltered. He followed her over with a low moan that might have been a word caught somewhere between lungs and lips, might have been nothing at all. They panted. Mya's heart banged against her ribs.

Quiet fell once more. Kayden sank into the mattress, and Mya slumped forward over him with a sigh. His hands still curled around her hips, gentle where they had been rough, thumb stroking over the curve of bone.

"You're beautiful," he said then, voice still gravel rumbling.

"And you're a tease," Mya retorted, smiling through the fall of her hair at him.

"Not a bit." Kayden tugged gently at the wrist that supported the weight of her body until she got the message and slid down to rest against his chest. "I followed through on every promise I made, lass. And then some."

That, Mya had to admit, was true enough. She chuckled, feeling him shiver a little with the wash of warm breath over skin still tingling with over sensitized nerve endings.

"You're a regular gentleman, Lieutenant McGregor."

"And you, Miss Boyle, are a man's dream come true."

She laughed again at that. "Flatterer."

"Only when it's called for."

His hand reached up, fingers sliding through her hair, and Mya let her eyes slide shut, leaning into the gentle touch. Carefully, she slid free of him, shifting so that she lay against his side. The silence between them felt warm, wrapped around her and holding her safe. Mya breathed in the scent of him, and let the silence settle.

Chapter 14

"Where were you?" Mya said into the quiet when they had lain in silence for long moments, the sounds of the convent become hospital a distant hum beyond the shield of the closed door. "When you were gone?"

She shifted as she spoke, curling herself closer to the warmth of his body, laying her head down on his shoulder. The dim light of the little paraffin lamp danced along his skin, drawing lines of shadow along the dip and rise of muscle beneath his skin. Mya lifted her eyes to his face.

"As soon as the shooting started, I had to find my men. I couldn't lie in a hospital bed while they were fighting. We were called to a site a few kilometers out of town," Kayden said, voice a vibration under her cheek, felt as much as heard. "There was, if you will believe it, some suspicion of a German spy having set up camp at one of the outlying farms." He sounded amused. "My unit is unattached now. We essentially rove about, doing whatever task we're put to, though our main duty here is to see that the setup of the hospital goes smoothly, and the injured and those caring for them are not put in any undo danger."

Mya traced a curling line over Kayden's stomach as he spoke, idly following some subconscious pattern. She nodded against his chest to show that she was still listening.

"After the mess of the other night, however, they apparently decided we'd serve better searching for spies. So, we did. For three days. Of course, we found nothing, though we did at least have a chance to aid in cleaning up what the bombing left behind." He shook his head, the smile completely gone from his voice. "Too many families have been damaged by the air strikes. Truthfully, if I had my choice, I would be up there stopping them head to head, but I'm not a pilot, so I have to do what I can down here."

"I'm sure that's more than enough," Mya said. "You saved my life. That must count for something."

He sighed, but his arm tightened around her. "I suppose I did."

There was quiet then, stretching between them in a way that wasn't entirely comfortable. It seemed to Mya that words left unsaid were piling up in the space, crowding at the corners of her mouth. She pushed them back. There would be a time for that. Though... She supposed she might test the waters, so to speak. Her eyes flicked briefly up toward Kayden's face. She couldn't see enough to guess at his mood, but she supposed a subject change was in order. He likely would not mind.

"Do you think?" she asked, letting her head tip down to rest again against his chest, her fingers still absently stroking over the flat expanse of his belly. "That it's entirely impossible that you knew me before?"

Kayden shifted up a little onto his elbow, looking down at her with his eyebrows drawn together over eyes that were shockingly dark in the lamplight, full of pooling shadows and secrets Mya couldn't decipher.

"Anywhere." She shrugged. "That you don't remember me doesn't mean we never crossed paths." She looked up at him. "Maybe I noticed you somewhere, though you didn't notice me, and that's why I feel as though I know you. Why I dream of your face." Her voice dipped low on the last words, her gaze dropping once more to his chest, and she was suddenly not sure whether she ought to have said them or not. Would he think she was strange? She had wondered as much herself, in the days he was gone. Of course, she had asked him when they met if he was her husband or her lover; it wasn't likely she could get much stranger than that.

"I suppose there's a small chance," Kayden said. "But I can't say I think it very likely." He was quiet for a moment, and Mya wondered if that would be the end of the discussion. Maybe there was nothing left to say. The dreams were her own, and it could just be that there was no explanation for them after all. Maybe she had just hit her head too hard. But try as she might to accept that, somewhere deep inside she knew it was wrong. "Although, I never got to finish what I was telling you earlier. Before the shell, and everything that came after. Which is that, in truth, I don't remember either."

Mya froze for only an instant, startled still, and then she rolled slightly so she could see his face. "You don't remember what?"

"I don't remember my past," he said, his turn to look away, not quite meeting her gaze. "I remember more of it than you do, of course. I remember Scotland. I remember home. But I don't remember being young. I just found myself there one day, walking through the hills with no clothes, nothing."

"Just like me," Mya said, her heart suddenly beating faster in her chest.

"I seem to remember you wearing clothes when I found you," Kayden said. "I think I would have noticed if that was otherwise."

"Well, I found a dress in the house, and I put it on." Mya laughed a little. "I didn't think it was really a good idea to go running about in a war zone naked."

"A sound decision." She could hear the smile in his voice.

"But when I woke up in that place, I wasn't wearing anything at all. I mean, what are the odds of that? That we both wake up with no memory, and no clothes. And then that we meet each other? That must be why I keep dreaming about you." She leaned up on her elbow, looking down at him, her words coming quick and excited. "I must have known you before. And you knew me. And the reason that you didn't think that you did is because you didn't remember me. The same as I don't remember you. But how could you, when you've forgotten your life just as much as I have mine?"

Kayden frowned, and Mya wondered if she had said something wrong. She withdrew a little, waiting for him to say something.

"I don't think so, lass" he said finally.

"What?" Mya stared at him. "Why? What is there to stop you from believing it?"

"You were right about the odds," he said quietly, "of us both waking up without our memories. And then running into each other. That's difficult enough to fathom. But if you add to that the idea that we knew each other before, it just becomes nearly impossible. It's far too much coincidence to make any kind of sense. I don't think it could happen."

"It's no coincidence," Mya said, her throat suddenly tight.

"No?" Kayden looked up at her with those dark eyes that made her knees feel weak every time she considered them. "What is it, then?"

"What if it's destiny?" Mya saw his expression start to shift, and rushed on before he had a chance to speak. "Hear me out before you say anything else. Maybe some people are just meant to be together. You know. Some people are just... soul mates."

"Soul mates?" Kayden sounded like he was trying not to laugh. "I'm sorry, Mya, but you know how ridiculous that idea is, right?"

"No. I don't think it's ridiculous at all. I think that it makes perfect sense." She set her jaw, her eyes narrowing. "What's so ridiculous about it?"

The laughter left his expression, and he looked up at her with a frown that was more confused than anything else. "Soul mates? The idea that somewhere out there you have someone who is waiting for you. I just don't know if I can be buying it, to be honest. It's a bit far-fetched."

"How can you not?" Mya asked. "I mean, I've been dreaming about you. And we shared the same dream. We—Everything that's happened. You happening to be there right at the right time to rescue me when you had no idea that I would be in that building. How can you not believe in soul mates?"

He shook his head. "A lot of that is just coincidence. I can't explain the dream thing, but maybe it had something to do with me getting you out of that building. It was just the way that our minds happened to interpret it."

"They both just happened to interpret it the same way?" Mya gave him a look that she hoped conveyed just how skeptical she was. "You think that it's too much of a coincidence that we both knew each other before we lost our memories, even though— might I mention—we've the same accent, meaning we came from the same region, if not the same town. So, that's far-fetched, but not that you and I had the same dream because our minds processed an event the same way, right down to the time line of the dream? And what about the fact that in my dream the person running beside me was my lover?"

"It's just not—" He sighed. "Can you just drop it, Mya? Please."

"Fine." Mya rolled off him, turning to face away. Behind her, she heard him shift like he might try to draw her back, but then he gave up, settling back down with another quiet sigh. She scowled at the empty bed across from her. She didn't understand how he couldn't agree with her when he'd seen the same things she had. But that was men, wasn't it? Had to have empirical proof for everything. And stubborn to boot, though maybe that was to Kayden.

She closed her eyes, ignoring the chill at her back where the gulf of mattress separated them, and tried to sleep.

Chapter 15

Sleep was not swift in coming. In fact, it wouldn't come for Mya at all.

Though Kayden's breathing had evened out behind her, Mya was restless. She wondered if he truly slept, or if he just thought to make her believe that he did. Her thoughts turned in restless circles, running along the same well-worn paths they had been tracing since she woke up in a home that was not her own to the sounds of bombs falling outside.

What if Kayden was right?

When sleep came at last, it brought dreams with it, as vivid as though she lived them.

In the dream, she woke, and she lay in the grass under a sky filled with stars. The moonlight spilled down over her, painting her bare skin with silver. The stag was there, white against the darkness. Time shifted and blurred. She saw Kayden, bow raised, heard her own voice, speaking a denial. The stars turned overhead, and the stag was gone. She stood on her feet, looking across the clearing, meeting Kayden's eyes. His dark hair was long, falling around his shoulders, and he wore a kilt.

A little late, Mya remembered that she was naked and covered herself with her hands, her cheeks flushing hot.

"I've already seen everything you're trying to hide just now," the man said—Kayden said—white teeth flashing in the dark, eyes sliding over her body.

"Well then you can stop looking, can't you?"

He laughed, a low, rough chuckle that went straight to somewhere in the center of her, warming her up from the inside out. "Aye. I suppose I could at that. And while I'm at it, maybe you can explain to me why you went chasing my hunt off."

"I told you," Mya said, wrapping her right arm a little closer around her chest.

"And if that's your real excuse then you're dumber than you look, running about the woods naked at the turn of the season, more than likely to freeze yourself to death."

"That wasn't exactly a choice," Mya answered, glaring at him.

"No? Then what exactly might it have been?"

"I..." Mya's eyebrows drew together. "I don't actually remember."

"You don't remember?"

"I don't know how I got here."

"So you show up, with no idea of how you've arrived or why you're here, naked as the day you were born, and your first instinct is to chase off the stag that would have fed me for the winter?"

Mya gave the thought a moment's consideration. "Yes."

"You're utterly crazy, woman."

"I can hardly be blamed for losing my memory."

"No. Nor for the craziness, I imagine," he said, and Mya glared at him.

"You're the one standing there, still staring at me," she pointed out. "If you think I'm so crazy, what are you hanging around for?"

"Mostly making sure you don't get yourself killed," he said. "A find man I'd be if I left some naked woman out in the woods to die alone."

"Yes. You're such a great help," Mya snapped. "Doing absolutely nothing except eying me up. What a gentleman."

"Losing your memory doesn't seem to have had any effect on the sharpness of your tongue."

"And what excuse do you have for your attitude?"

"You. Chasing off my dinner." He slid the arrow he was still holding back into the quiver and unstrung his bow, slinging it over his shoulder. "That would make any man a little less than polite."

"If it's that great a deal to you, I'll cook you a dinner, for god's sake."

"With just what, pray tell?" He raised an eyebrow at her as he stepped in closer. "And can you even cook? You say you have no memory of why you showed up here in this field. What makes you think you would know your way around a kitchen?"

Mya thought about it, then lifted one shoulder in a shrug and let it fall again. "I just feel like I would. At least enough to get by."

"Do you even know your own name?"

"Mya." She spoke slowly, tasting the word that had just come to her on her tongue. Yes. That was right. "My name is Mya."

The night slid into darkness, and then there was light in her eyes, painting the backs of her eyelids red. Mya opened them to the room in the convent.

She almost imagined, as she blinked up at the high ceiling with its white, cracked plaster, that she could still smell the scent of grass, soft and green beneath her. Could still feel the breeze that moved across her skin, prickling goosebumps in its chill wake. But of course, neither were there. Kayden still slept beside her, his chest rising and falling in easy rhythm. The smell of him filled her senses, warm and rich, heavy over the lighter scent of the linen that draped the bed. She thought of waking him. Of her hands against his skin and his mouth on her body, but he had been three days on patrol, and she could not bring herself to disturb his rest.

She was not sure, anyway, that she knew what she wished to say to him after their conversation the night before. Whether she wished to admit that he had been right. She wasn't even sure, yet, if she thought he had been. But she could see his point of view. Could understand it. If someone had come to her saying that they were destined for each other, would she have believed them if she hadn't been the one having the dreams? The rationalization didn't lessen the ache in her chest.

Reluctantly, she slid from the bed, moving carefully so that she would not wake him. She too special care with the blankets, folding them back just enough to slip free and dropping her feet over the edge of the bed. The floor was cold, and she hurried across it to her little broken chest, pulling a pair of thick socks from the little stack of clothing inside and drawing them on. Underwear and pants followed, and then she took the clean shirt out and began buttoning it up, trying to ignore the way she kept imagining Kayden's hands there, the ghosts of last night's rushed disrobing.

When she was clothed, she tied her boots on and ventured out into the rest of the building. There were soldiers to be tended to. Work to be done. She still had that, whatever else came. It was something of a comfort, to know that she was useful. That there was some point in her being at the convent, and that she was not just dead weight.

Men in uniform hurried past as she made her way down the corridor, each of them no doubt going somewhere important. A few of them—the friendlier ones, or the men she had met personally in the days that Kayden was gone—stopped to smile at her. Others seemed completely unaware of her presence. It was a strange feeling. As though she didn't exist at all. She thought of getting some breakfast, but it was likely that there would be men getting theirs, and Mya wasn't sure that she wanted to walk into the mess hall alone in front of all of them, thought she would prefer not existing to having that many curious eyes on her. Thus, far she had taken food in her room, or in rushed moments between patients. There had been no time for the mess when it was busy with men. Mya sighed, and decided against another visit there just yet. She would have to brave it eventually; she didn't think there was much chance that she could avoid regular eating hours forever, but she would prefer to do the braving with Kayden by her side. If Kayden had any desire to be by her side any longer.

She was, she admitted to herself, perhaps being a little bit over dramatic.

That Kayden didn't believe in soul mates did not mean that he did not want her still. Even if he thought her perhaps a little touched in the head. She did have the excuse of the recent injury, after all. Whether he would take a different position if she continued to feel the same way, Mya wasn't certain, but she had to believe that he would not just toss her aside after what they had shared.

She was no swooning maiden, but what had passed between them the night before had been special. Even Kayden had to have felt it. The energy. The connection. She had known his body, and he had known hers. There was no way to deny that. Whether one called it luck or perhaps something else didn't matter. What mattered was the truth of it.

Mya brushed a lock of hair that seemed determined to escape its ties back behind her ear, sighing. Of course, if Kayden did not accept the truth that she knew to exist, she could not say that was all that mattered, could she? She shook her head. It seemed that off late all her thoughts simply ran in circles, coming back to the same questions. Her memories could have answered them, but she did not have those. The dreams told her something, but what she was quite sure yet. They remained too cryptic, the memories in them too scattered to explain her past. To tell her what direction her path might lead.

"Well, well," a voice said ahead of her. "If it isn't the doctor's errand girl."

She knew that voice.

Mya lifted her head to meet the eyes of the man who owned it, the one who had been less than kind to her on the first day that Kayden had been missing, when she had made an official decision to do something more functional with herself than sit in the room and mope.

"Good morning," she said, keeping her tone cordial. The last thing she wanted was to deal with someone who was going to be rude simply because he was too lazy to be anything else.

"Is it?" The man laughed. "Are you sure about that, Miss Boyle?"

"I am, actually," Mya said, lifting her chin and continuing her path, though it would bring her within arm's reach of him. She was not going to be intimidated into tucking tail and taking a different route through the convent. If he wished to frighten someone, he would have to look elsewhere. She wasn't so sure that it was exactly shaping up to be a good morning, but that didn't matter; she didn't feel like sharing the private inner workings of her life with him, so as far as he was concerned she was having a wonderful day.

There was just something about him that put her off. Something hidden beneath the almost blank expression he'd adopted. She had noted it from the moment she met him, and nothing in their brief encounters since had done anything to change her opinion.

"I'm glad to hear it, then," he said, and Mya was certain that was a lie. He didn't care whether she was happy or not. Why should he?

Mya nodded once, a silent, brusque thanks for his interest. A few more steps and she would be past him, and free to go on her way.

"I hear that Lieutenant McGregor has returned," he said as they neared each other.

"Aye," Mya said, darting a furtive glance down the hall in hopes of finding someone to rescue her from conversation with him, but the corridor was empty except for the two of them. She was sure it had been busy just a moment before, which was entirely unfair.

"Unharmed, I hope?"

"More or less."

She was beginning to be fed up with his nosing into her life. Though his tone was friendly, something in it made the skin along her spine crawl, and she had no desire to remain alone with him.

"It seems you two are quite close," he said, not even attempting to disguise his prodding. "Exceptionally so, some might say. "

"We're sharing a sick room because we were both brought in at the same time," Mya said. "And it was the room available. Beyond that, I'm sure that rumor has come up with any number of delightful things, but just because you heard someone say it doesn't mean it's true."

"Oh, come now," Lachlan said. "You don't expect me to believe that one, do you, lass?"

"Believe whatever you want," Mya said, moving to step past him. "I hardly care."

His arm shot out, and his fingers curled around her bicep, holding in a tight grip.

Chapter 16

Mya gave the unwanted hand on her body a withering glance. "I'll thank you to let me go. Right *now*."

"Oh, I don't think so." The big hand tightened, the red-haired man looking down at her with something like hunger behind the hard light in his eyes. "You haven't answered my questions."

The world flickered.

For a moment, Mya was somewhere else. Some *when* else, and the man in front of her was looming over her from the back of a horse, bearded and clad in a kilt. His smile was cruel.

"I think not," he'd said. "I'm still talking to you."

Behind the familiar-unfamiliar form, she could see, superimposed like a double exposed photograph, the clean-shaven soldier from her own time. He spoke but she didn't hear him. The voice ringing in her ears was her own, echoing through the memory. From a time before now.

"Take your hands off me!" Mya bit the words out, yanking against his grip, the wind whipping through her hair, no longer in the convent hospital. The man's hand didn't loosen. "I'm a betrothed woman!"

"You say that," Lachlan said. "But I don't know that I actually believe it." His horse pranced nervously in place, and Mya tried again to pull away, avoiding the hooves. "You see, girl, you're not wearing a ring on your finger. I've heard nothing about wedding plans. No bakers hired. No seamstress making a dress. And Kayden hasn't introduced you to the clan. He's kept you shut away in that house since you arrived, and yet you want me to believe that you're engaged to the man?"

"I am," Mya said, forcing the words out past the tight constriction in her throat. "Ask him, if you don't believe me. He's kept me in the house to protect me. To be near me. Take me home, and we'll talk to him when he arrives."

Lachlan laughed. "No," he said. "I don't think so."

Before she had a chance to protest, he was leaning down, reaching for her—

"Are you daft, woman?"

The vision dissolved, and she was standing again in the hallway of the convent, Lachlan's hand wrapped painfully around her arm. Anger swept through her.

"Am *I* daft?" She edged the question with laughter. "This asked by the man who grabbed me without my consent and refuses to release me."

"You—"

"I what?" Mya interrupted. "I won't answer your questions? What I do with Kayden McGregor is frankly none of your damn business, and your attempt to make it so has only succeeded in making me exceedingly angry. I suggest you let go of my arm. *Now.*"

His grip only tightened. He didn't speak.

Mya didn't give him time to. The choice he'd made was obvious. Jaw clenched tight, she spun on her heel and slammed her elbow into the space just below his ribs.

He dropped her, wheezing.

"In the future," Mya said, drawing herself up to her full height and looking down at him where he was hunched over, the air driven from his lungs. "I'll thank you not to lay your hands on me."

He snarled, and moved like he would grab her again, but Mya sidestepped his reaching hand. The last time, she thought, there had been a sword. She'd made him bleed with it. The image was just at the edge of her thoughts, vague and uncertain, but she was sure of it. If he touched her again, she'd see about recreating the experience.

"Bitch," he said under his breath as she turned away.

Mya's jaw tightened, but she didn't look back. He'd caused her enough grief. She wasn't going to give him the satisfaction of letting him know that she'd heard him. Let him mutter uselessly to himself if he liked. It wasn't her problem.

"Is that any way to speak to a woman?"

She hadn't heard anyone else approaching, but the man who had just come around the corner and was currently staring Lachlan down must have heard them, because he looked less than pleased.

Mya turned just enough to watch the confrontation over her shoulder, curious to see how Lachlan would respond.

"No," he huffed. "Sir."

A commanding officer, then. Mya swallowed a smile. Even better. If he knew men with authority were keeping tabs on him, maybe Lachlan would leave her alone.

"No," the tall man repeated. "I didn't think so. Don't let me hear it happening again, or you'll be getting latrine duty."

"Of course, sir."

Lachlan hurried off, and Mya watched him go with a swell of satisfaction. It might have been even stronger if she'd chased him off herself, but she wasn't going to look a gift horse in the mouth.

"Thank you," she said when he was out of sight and presumably out of hearing.

"Of course, Miss." The man shot a disapproving glance in the direction that Lachlan had gone. "I don't allow my men to treat anyone with disrespect. Least of all those who are giving their time to the war effort."

The war effort. Mya hadn't thought of it that way, but she supposed running errands for the doctor and doing what little she could around the convent to help the wounded and make life easier for those who stayed there counted as aiding in it.

"I help where I'm able," Mya said. "It's hardly a great contribution."

"Even a small contribution is something." The officer smiled. He was, Mya noted, rather handsome, with neatly combed blond hair and sharp blue eyes. "That you attempt to help matters. I've seen you with the men." His voice softened. "You're good with them. They need that."

"You're very kind to say so," Mya said. She paused, uncertain whether she ought to ask his name or not.

"Captain Taylor," he said, obviously guessing the source of her uncertainty. "If you need anything, please feel free to let me know. And if Lachlan bothers you again, I'll make quite certain he's sorry for it."

"I appreciate that," Mya said. "More than you know. Thank you."

He frowned. "I hope that he hasn't bothered you before. Has this been ongoing?"

"No. No." Mya shook her head. "I've hardly seen him before today. He wasn't exactly friendly before, but this was the first encounter of the sort I had with him. And I'm sure there won't be another one."

"I'll see to it that there isn't." Captain Taylor moved to turn, and paused. "Is there anything else I can do for you?"

"Thank you," Mya said. "For the help and for the offer. But I think I can do well enough on my own now that he's gone."

"Then I shall leave you to it. Have a good night, Miss Boyle."

He went off down the hall, footfalls even as a metronome beat, and Mya wondered if that was something all soldiers picked up with time. That marching gait with its perfect four/four time. She laughed a little at herself for the thought. Kayden didn't walk like that. But she didn't know how long he'd been in the military. Maybe it was something that only happened after a certain number of years.

She shook her head, then, and pushed herself into action. Standing in the hall wasn't going to get anything done, and she had duties to fulfill. Humming cheerfully to herself, she started off down the corridor toward the occupied wing of the hospital.

Chapter 17

When Mya returned to the room that night, Kayden was already there, apparently having decided against staying with his regiment. She hesitated in the doorway, uncertain how to speak to him. The disagreement of the night before might not have chased him away, but that didn't mean that he'd completely forgotten about it.

The lamp was lit, and its flickering glow moved over his face, highlighting the elegant arches of his cheekbones and darkening his eyes. Mya found herself staring, mesmerized by the sight. She wanted to be angry at him, but found whatever resentment had been building start to melt away. She inhaled silently, trying to prepare herself for whatever he might have to say. Kayden had to know she was there, but he didn't look up from the boot he had balanced on his knee, shining it with quick, efficient motions.

"Good evening," Mya said finally, dragging her gaze from the way that his hands moved in the lamplight. She quietly stepped into the room.

"Good evening, Mya," Kayden answered.

With the door closed behind her and the blackout curtains drawn, the room became their own little closed off sanctuary. An island amid the chaos of the convent-made-hospital and the war that raged outside. She leaned against the wall and folded her hands in front of her. "Did you have a pleasant day?" The words felt stilted and awkward as they left her tongue, and she hoped he couldn't hear the uncertainty in them.

"It was pleasant enough, I suppose." For a moment he said nothing. Mya wondered if she had somehow missed something.

Was he angry with her? He still hadn't looked up from the boot. "How was yours?"

"Uneventful, for the most part," Mya answered. "I had a bit of a run in with..." She paused, not sure how to describe Lachlan. "Another one of the men."

Kayden's hands went still. "What kind of run in?" he demanded, lifting his head to look at her like he was searching her for injuries. He set the boot aside. "Were you hurt?"

"No." Mya shook her head, stepping forward without thought to lay a hand on his shoulder. She caught herself and stopped. Moved instead to her bed she sank down on the edge of it. "He didn't hurt me."

"Who was it?" Kayden's voice had dropped lower, harsh and verging on angry. She could see the tension in his jaw and his shoulders. "What happened?"

Mya took a breath and let it out again. "He said his name is Lachlan."

Kayden's hands curled into fists against his thighs. "I ought to have known," he said coldly.

"Does he make a habit of accosting women, then?" Mya asked.

Kayden barked a laugh. "Not so much accosting women as trying to make my life difficult. He must have targeted you because he's seen you with me." He shook his head. "I'm sorry, Mya."

Mya waved the apology away. "Don't be. It's hardly your fault that he decided to behave like a child. He grabbed my arm and tried to get me to talk to him about our relationship."

"He *grabbed* you?" Kayden was up off the bed and halfway to the door before Mya leapt up to follow him.

She caught his arm, gently, and tugged him back toward her. "Don't. Please. You'll only get in trouble."

The look on Kayden's face said he was sure it would be worth it, but Mya didn't want him disciplined for her sake. "Please," she said again

Kayden's shoulder's slumped, and he sighed. He turned slowly back to face her.

"He didn't actually hurt me." Mya smiled a little ruefully. "I think if anyone was hurt, actually, it was him. I elbowed him rather hard."

"He deserved it," Kayden said, but some of the anger had gone from his voice, and he let her lead him back to the bed to sit down.

"Anyway," Mya continued, "Captain Taylor saw some of what happened, and he stepped in. I don't think Lachlan will be speaking to me out of order again."

"Captain Taylor," Kayden said slowly.

Mya's eyebrows drew together in a confused frown. "Yes," she said. "Captain Taylor. He might have heard some of the struggle. I'm not sure. But he came around the corner just as Lachlan was muttering some pretty unflattering things, and he told him that if he caught him being so disrespectful again he'd make sure he got latrine duty." She smiled at the memory of Lachlan's face when he'd heard the words. "The Captain was very kind to me, too. He thanked me for helping with the war effort."

"Helping with the war effort?" Kayden gave her a questioning look. Beneath it, she could still see lingering tension, but she didn't push. So long as he didn't actually run off and attack Lachlan, she wasn't going to try and stop him being angry.

"While you were gone I started working as the doctor's assistant. Mostly I file paperwork and carry things, but it's something to do."

He was quiet for a moment, thoughtful. "So you like Captain Taylor, then?"

Mya was a little surprised by the sudden shift back to the captain. "Yes," she said, feeling as though the question was leading somewhere and not quite sure where that was.

"He's a good man," Kayden said.

And that was that. He didn't say anything else. Didn't even look at her again. He just moved back to his bed and picked up the boot he'd been polishing, while Mya stared after him, perplexed.

Did she like Captain Taylor? What kind of a question was that? He'd helped her, been nice to her, it was hardly a crime to like someone who appreciated your efforts. What was Kayden's—*Oh!* The reason for the question was so obvious she was kind of ashamed she hadn't figured it out immediately.

"Kayden," she said quietly.

He grunted an acknowledgment without looking up at her and Mya nearly laughed.

"I appreciate that Captain Taylor was kind to me, and that he made sure Lachlan wouldn't bother me again. Nothing more than that." She put a little extra emphasis on the *nothing*.

Kayden's motions slowed. He looked up. Mya met his gaze, trying not to let the giggle that was building in her chest escape. "Truly," she said. "That's it."

"Well, it's hardly my business if you like him for something more than that."

Mya did laugh then. "Whether it's your business or not, you obviously want it to be," she said, a teasing lilt to her voice. "Were you truly jealous of him, after I slept in your arms last night?"

There was no answer.

Kayden stared hard at the shoe in his hand. Mya shook her head. *Men.* Unbelievable.

"You have nothing to be jealous of," she said, just in case he hadn't gathered that the first time she'd explained it. It was hard to tell sometimes.

"I'm not jealous," Kayden said.

Mya snorted. "Right. You were absolutely not jealous of Captain Taylor and his perfectly coiffed blond hair in any way."

"What do I have to be jealous of?" Kayden said. "Yes, we shared a bed last night, but that does not mean I have some exclusive claim to you. You're not an object to be owned." One corner of his mouth tipped up into a lopsided grin. "And my hair is much better than his."

"Oh, is it now?" Mya gave Kayden a long look, eyebrows lifted. "You know you both have the same haircut."

"You want me to be jealous," Kayden said. "Is that it, lass?"

"Do I want you to be jealous?" Mya tapped a finger against her lower lip, considering. "You think me pointing out that you have the same haircut because you serve on the same military force is a deliberate plot to make you jealous?"

Kayden's mouth moved like it wanted to curl into a smile, but he kept his expression even. He set the boot aside again. "I think," he said, rising slowly from the bed, "That I would not put it past you to do such a thing."

He prowled across the room as he spoke, dark eyes fixed on her, and Mya's throat went suddenly dry. She was all about missing obvious clues at the moment, it would seem, because what Kayden was getting at was about as subtle as a slap in the face.

"You know how I am," she said, tipping her head back to look up into his eyes as he moved in closer. "Always trying to see how much I can rile a man up."

The low chuckle that answered her words made Mya's stomach tighten with want.

"Admit it." His voice was low and hungry. "You like me riled."

Mya had to agree, as he drew her to him, that she did.

Chapter 18

Mya woke to Kayden's arm around her waist, and his breath warm against the nape of her neck.

It was dark in the room, the blackout curtains still drawn from the night before, blocking out the light of the sun that would otherwise be spilling through the window. Beneath the blankets, it was warm, and the mattress was soft. Kayden was solid and safe at her back. For a moment Mya considered allowing herself to sink back down into dreams. She had been dreaming of... something. The visuals escaped her when she reached for them, slipping out of reach and leaving only vague impressions of soft fur and firelight behind. But it had been a good dream. Of that much she was certain.

Kayden stirred, and Mya smiled into the pillow when his arm tightened, drawing her closer against his chest. Their argument hadn't done any serious damage to the relationship beginning between them, if last night was anything to go on. She felt her cheeks heat a little at the memory, and was rather glad Kayden wasn't awake to see the stupid grin on her face.

It didn't matter, in that moment, that he didn't believe in destiny. That he thought the concept of soul mates was a ridiculous one. Mya could live with that, so long as he remained by her side. She didn't need the promise of endless lifetimes. Just this one, right here, and she couldn't imagine a better way to spend it than in Kayden's arms.

As though his attention was summoned by her thoughts, Kayden roused himself, and brushed his lips against the knob of her spine where it sat under the thin skin just above her shoulder blades.

"Morning," he said, voice rough with sleep.

"Good morning to you too," Mya answered, lazy smile in the words.

He chuckled at her obvious satisfaction. "I take it you slept well, then, lass?"

"Mmm." Mya uncurled from his arms, stretching long and leisurely. "Very well. Thank you." She rolled to face him, looking up into warm dark eyes still a little hazy with just waking, and he leaned down to steal a brief, almost chaste kiss. She curled a hand around the nape of his neck, fingers combing through the short-cropped hair. For the barest fraction of a second it felt strange, the ends against her skin. She had somehow expected it to be longer. But the disorientation faded almost before she could recognize it for what it was, and she smiled up at him. "And you? Did you sleep well?"

His arm tightened around her waist. "I couldn't have slept better in the king's own bed."

As far as Mya was concerned, they could have stayed like that forever, wrapped up in each other in the warm safety of their little room, letting the world outside go its own way. But there were things that had to be done. Kayden had his duties and she had hers. She sighed softly, letting her head drop to rest against his shoulder.

"Do you have to go?"

He was a moment in answering, fumbling around for something that turned out to be his watch. Mya lifted her gaze to watch his face as he read the time on it, and then he shook his head, setting it back down just under the edge of the pillow.

"No," he said, fingers tracing the dip of her spine up and down in the curve of her lower back. "I don't have to go just yet. Today is a rest day, with all we've been doing. If it doesn't stay quiet, I'm sure I'll be summoned, but until then, I've some time."

"Stay with me, then?" Mya requested. "The doctor can do without me for the morning. He's certainly done it before."

Kayden's hand smoothed over her hair. "I'll stay as long as you like, lass. There's nowhere I'd rather be right at this moment, than here in bed with you."

Beyond their walls, Mya could faintly hear the sounds of the convent waking for the day. Boots in the hall. The sound of trucks idling outside. But she paid none of it any attention.

"How did you find yourself in the military?" she asked, hoping Kayden wouldn't mind the question; she wanted to know a little more about the man she was sharing a room with. They'd hardly had time to talk before, and she intended to take full advantage of the moment.

"When I... woke up, I suppose, in Scotland, I had no memory, as I've mentioned before. I knew my name and not much else." A smile slipped into his voice. "But it seemed the name was enough. There were some McGregors local to the area, and they took me in. Took care of me. Helped me get back on my feet. They were kind, but I knew that I could not remain with them forever. I had to find some means of making my own way in the world. Which I found in the military. I won't say it's an easy life, but it's one worth living."

"Will you stay in it, then?"

He paused, thoughtful, and then shook his head. "For a time, yes. Beyond that, I cannot say. I suppose it will depend on the state of the world. And on my own health. There is always a chance I will be wounded in action and unable to continue fighting. But my hope is that I will carry on here until I am satisfied that my work for them has been done. Then I will retire, and find some simple job in some shop or some such back home. Maybe find myself a lass. Have a babe or two."

You already have yourself a lass.

Mya caught the words on the tip of her tongue back. Kayden was under no obligation to consider her something permanent.

Or even steady. They had not known each other for even a fortnight. And though she felt as though she had known him before, as though he had always somehow been a part of her, Mya knew that Kayden did not feel the same way. It would take time to convince him, but Mya had that. She was willing to spend the rest of her life making him believe the truth, so long as she got to spend it with him.

"It's a good plan," she said instead. "A good life."

"And what of you?" Kayden asked. "When the war is done, or you are done here, what will you do?"

Follow him wherever he went, Mya thought. But that might not be an answer he was ready to hear. "Return to Scotland, I suppose. Look for my family. Try to find out who I am." She tipped her head back to look up at him, a smile on her lips. "Find myself a great strapping Scotsman, maybe."

His hand curled a little closer around her hip, consciously or unconsciously possessive, and Mya stifled a laugh. So that was how it was to be, then. "Yes," she continued, just to see how much she could get him to admit. "A man, and a little house somewhere. Looking over water. With a warm fire in the hearth and a garden in the back."

What had started as teasing turned wistful as she went on, and Mya trailed off, biting her lip. She couldn't imagine anyone but Kayden by her side there, even in jest.

"Just so long," Kayden said. "As the man with you there is not Captain Taylor."

Startled, Mya laughed, and realized that the remark had been a deliberate attempt to break her out of the sudden silence that had taken her tongue. "What is it that you have against Captain Taylor, exactly?" she asked, leaning up on one elbow to look down at him. "Did he steal your girl or something?"

"He would if he could," Kayden said, looking up at her, and though there was laughter in his eyes, behind it Mya thought she could see something else. Some genuine emotion, earnest and claiming. But perhaps she was just seeing what she wanted to see there. Still, he had all but said she was his girl, just then. Had spoken in the present tense. Maybe it was just a joke. Mya didn't want it to be just a joke.

"You ought to safeguard her better, then," she said. "Bring her nylons or something."

"Nylons, hmm?"

"Or something," Mya repeated, trying not to laugh. "If you want to stop Captain Taylor from stealing your girl, you're going to have to give her reasons to stay, you know."

He growled at that, and suddenly they were moving, his hand on her hip turning her with him. A heartbeat later, Mya found herself flat against the mattress, looking up at Kayden. "I think I can come up with plenty of reasons for her to stay," he said. "Reasons far better than Nylons."

Mya's answering giggle was breathless, her heart racing in her chest. "I'm certain that you can."

He leaned down, then, so close that they were sharing breath. Her lips parted, waiting for the kiss. It never came.

"Corporal McGregor!" The call was accompanied by a heavy knocking on the door.

Kayden made a sound low in the back of his throat, irritation at being interrupted, and levered himself up and off Mya. "Give me a minute," he called back.

He grabbed his clothes from the chair in the corner and started pulling them on, while Mya watched from the bed, disappointed to see all that glorious skin be rapidly covered. She didn't bother getting up herself, just pulled the sheet higher around her shoulders and hoped that Kayden wouldn't open the door wide enough for the man outside to notice that she wasn't in her own bed.

"I'm sorry, Mya," Kayden said as he scooped up his hat and hurried toward the door. "I'll just be a moment."

She needn't have worried about being seen in bed. Kayden opened the door only wide enough that he could just slip through, and pulled it quickly shut behind him. It was a little suspicious, especially when he was sharing a room with a woman, but Mya supposed it was better than being caught outright. She didn't know what rules the military had about that sort of thing, but likely they existed, and she and Kayden weren't married.

Outside, she could hear their voices rising and falling, the individual words impossible to make out, and then fading away entirely, swallowed by distance. Mya sighed. It didn't seem as though Kayden would be coming back any time soon. Which meant that it was likely time for her to get out of bed and see if the doctor needed any errands run or paperwork filed.

Reluctantly, she hauled herself out of the warm nest that she'd been curled into, and went to her little chest to find something to wear. She was going to have to wash her clothes again soon. The last time had been while Kayden was away.

She pulled clothes out of the trunk and dressed, then ran her hands through her hair and braided it back from her face. It would have been nice, to have more time with Kayden. To talk to him, and learn more about him, but she supposed that would just have to wait now. With another soft sigh, she went to see where she could be of use.

The day was surprisingly quiet. Mya helped run a few things back and forth, but for the most part there was little to do. The men were resting peacefully, and there weren't any new wounded coming in just yet. Mya knew from what she'd heard the men saying there was no ground war in this part of France, though there was always a chance that could change at any moment. Mya had pushed any worry about such a thing aside. If the circumstance did change, there was hardly anything she could do about it, and until it did, worrying would only make her feel worse. So she'd made herself let go of any such concerns, and just deal with what was happening here in the moment. And at the moment, that was mostly making sure that there were clean sheets for everyone and that the doctor's files were organized.

Lunch came and went, and Mya decided to head back to her room for a break.

She hummed softly to herself as she walked, a song that she couldn't remember learning. It felt familiar, though, like something that she had once known well. If she reached, she could almost... But no, it was gone again, and Mya had to content herself with the melody. She nodded a friendly hello to the soldiers she passed in the hall, and a few of them smiled back.

When she reached the room, the door was just slightly open, as though someone had come in and not thought to close it entirely after themselves. As she stepped in, she realized the reason why.

Kayden was sitting cross legged on the floor, the chest in front of him. He had the lid off, and was fiddling with something that Mya realized after a moment were the hinges. She closed the door with a click, and he startled like he hadn't heard her enter the room, looking up from the project he'd been engrossed in.

"What are you doing?" Mya asked, curious.

"Fixing this," Kayden answered. He smiled at her. "Your hinges weren't put on properly, which is why it wasn't sitting straight. But I think I've managed to mostly deal with the problem. You should be able to actually close it now."

To demonstrate, he reattached the lid, and closed it. It sat straight. Mya stared at it until she realized that Kayden was probably waiting for her to say something, and that she was being terribly rude.

"Oh. I'm sorry." She stepped closer and went down on knee, inspecting the improvements. "This looks wonderful, Kayden. Thank you."

Her eyes lifted to his and she found him smiling, more than a little pleased with himself.

"It was hardly anything," he said.

"It was something," Mya answered. "And it was kind of you to think of me." She smiled. "And it's nice to know that no one is going to be getting any accidental glimpse of my things."

Kayden laughed at that. "You don't have anything in there we haven't seen before," he pointed out. "The uniform clothes are the same ones the men wear."

"There's just something about privacy," Mya said, dropping back to sit beside him, cross-legged too. "I find that I'm quite fond of it."

"I suppose I shouldn't mention that I saw your underwear, then," Kayden said, turning to look at her with a badly stifled grin.

Mya swatted his shoulder. "You've seen my underwear already anyway. I wore them in front of you. More than once."

Kayden's eyes danced with mirth. "I think," he said slowly, holding her gaze. "That I like them better in the trunk."

Chapter 19

Cheeks flushing red, Mya shoved Kayden hard enough that his balance wavered a little, almost sending him toppling over. She didn't think her glare was quite a success, though; she was trying too hard not to laugh.

"That's a terrible thing to say."

"Terrible? Hardly. I just think you look better without them." He reached out as he spoke, curling his fingers into the waistband of her pants and drawing her forward.

Mya found herself abruptly half in his lap, one of his arms wrapped around her waist, the other hand reaching down to unbutton her trousers.

"You see," he said as he pulled down the zipper. "If you weren't wearing underwear, things would be so much easier for me."

Warmth coiled through Mya's limbs, settling in her stomach, and she took in a sharp little breath through her teeth as he reached down lower and brushed his fingers over her clit through the thin fabric of the undergarments.

"I can see that," she said, breath catching on the words.

"Then you see," he said. "Why you ought not to wear them."

Even as he growled the words into her ear, he was slipping his hand inside the panties, fingers brushing against her clit on their way. Mya let her head fall back against Kayden's shoulder with a gasp.

"I think," she said, forcing the words out past the moan that wanted to escape. "You're doing j-just fine with them on."

"True," Kayden agreed, fingertips rubbing circles around her entrance. "But just think how much better it would be if you weren't wearing them."

Mya didn't have it in her to attempt to argue his logic, as long as he kept doing that. She reached for the hand that wasn't busy between her thighs, curling her fingers around his wrist for something to hold onto.

"You're so unbelievably lovely," he said against her hair, voice rough.

"Kayden," Mya breathed.

One of his fingers slid inside her. Her spine arched against his chest, her body rocking up into the press of it. The heel of his hand rubbed against her clit, and Mya rolled her hips, trying to get more of that sensation, chasing the pleasure.

"I love the way you feel against me. Love how desperate you get," Kayden said the words, sending exquisite shivers down the length of Mya's spine. "I love watching you fall apart, Mya. You do it so beautifully."

He pulled back, and one finger became two. He couldn't take her the way she wanted, though, his reach too constricted by her clothing, and as much as Mya tried she couldn't have him deeper. Couldn't have him filling her completely. She whined through her teeth, nails leaving marks in the skin of his wrist where her fingers tightened.

"Having trouble?" Kayden inquired, his voice quietly amused.

"Damn it, Kayden. Just—" The word broke off into a cry as he shifted his hand, rocking it hard against her nub.

"Just what?" He nipped at the shell of her ear. "Tell me what you want, darling. Anything in my power, I'll give it to you."

"I want you to get these clothes off me." Mya writhed in his lap. He was hard beneath her, and he groaned when she rolled the curve of her backside deliberately against his length.

His fingers pulled out, and Mya made a low sound of disappointment, but she didn't have long to wait. An instant later he was stripping her out of pants and underwear, not even bothering with the shirt she still wore, and laying her out on the bed. His own clothes rapidly discarded, he followed.

Mya cried his name as he pressed one hand over her hip, holding her down against the mattress, and filled her again with his fingers. Her toes curled against the blanket, her thighs falling open for his touch.

"Yes," he said. "Just like that. Just like that for me."

She reached up and pulled him down to her, arching into a kiss that he was more than happy to share. Both hands curled around the back of his neck, thumbs stroking over the muscle there.

The kiss grew long and languid, Kayden's tongue exploring every inch of her mouth. His fingers slowed to match the pace. Mya felt as though she ought to mind somehow, but the desperation that had been building a moment before had softened into something else. Something that wanted as much of Kayden as she could have—his skin against hers, his mouth, his hands.

She just wanted him.

All of him.

Forever.

When they parted, Kayden brushed his lips against the curve of her jaw, and then downward, along her throat. Mya tipped her head back to give him space, a moan slipping from her mouth as his fingers rubbed against that place inside her that made pleasure shock down her thighs and up into her belly.

"Kayden..."

"I'm here," he said, as though he knew what she wanted. Knew exactly what she needed. But he had, hadn't he? He had since the first moment they'd fallen into bed together. "I'm here, darling."

She arched into him, trying to draw him closer. To have more of him. His kisses moved further down, over her breastbone and then back up again, his mouth finding hers.

How could he touch her like this, Mya wondered as he settled over her, and not understand what she meant when she said they were soul mates? He had to be able to feel the connection between them, buzzing like electricity over her skin. Mya breathed his name against his mouth, and Kayden groaned, the kiss deepening.

"I want you," she said when they were panting against each other's lips, his forehead resting against hers. "Kayden. Please."

"Yes," he said. He drew his fingers back again, stroking one last time against the place inside her on the way out, and then his hands were turning her gently, his body pressing against hers.

Mya sobbed something that might have been his name as he guided her leg back over his hip, opening her to him, and slid inside.

Like this, her back to his chest, her head against his bicep and his arm curled over her chest, the rhythm they shared was slow and easy. Mya could feel every inch of him pressed to her, his skin warm against her own, and it was perfect. It was exactly what she needed.

The hand that had been on her thigh slid down, thumb rubbing over her clit, and Mya turned her head so that Kayden could lean down over her and claim her mouth once more. Like that, connected all the way down, they moved together, and Mya felt release building in the core of her, slowly pulling her tight with need. It was deep, and lingering, and not at all rushed, a slow swell of pleasure that would break into a wave at its height.

She reached up, wrapping her arm around to sink her fingers into his hair. The other lay over his, fingers laced together against her shoulder.

"Mya," Kayden said when they parted. "Mya."

It was as though all he could remember was her name. He said it like she was something precious, like the word felt holy in his mouth, and Mya felt her chest tighten with something that wasn't pleasure at all. It was need, but not physical, love and aching longing.

"Yes," Mya said, and what she meant was *I love you*.

The pleasure that had been building, rolling slowly along her limbs to pool at her center, was suddenly urgent, the rising need for release coming at last to its peak. Mya caught at Kayden's hand, holding tight, and he must have felt it because he rocked his thumb down hard over her clit. She was shuddering against him, spine pulling into a curve and thighs trembling. The wild crest of the pleasure rushed through her, filling her up and washing her clean of anything but Kayden. His body against hers, his hands on her skin. She heard him muffle a groan as he followed her over the edge, his teeth sinking into her shoulder just hard enough to make her gasp his name, hips hitching and body sparking with aftershocks. His arms held her close.

"I love you," Mya said, the words slipping from her mouth before she could hold them back. "Dammit, Kayden. I love you."

Chapter 20

Mya realized, as she slumped back against Kayden, her heart still beating too fast against her ribs, what she had said. Kayden hadn't spoken. Her heart sank.

"I..." She wasn't sure where the words were going. Maybe an apology. A plea that he not let her slip ruin the moments they had just shared.

"You don't need to be sorry," Kayden said behind her before she could finish.

Mya big her lip, blinking back the sting of tears. She wasn't going to cry in front of him.

Kayden stroked a hand over her hip and down the outside of her thigh, back up again. "You never need to apologize for loving someone." He brushed a kiss against her hair. "Not even when they don't love you back, Mya. It is hardly your fault, what you feel. And it isn't... It is not a bad thing, to love."

Not sure she trusted her voice, Mya just shook her head, wondering how they had ended up here, having this conversation in this moment, when they had been so perfect just minutes before.

"I do care about you," Kayden said. "I care about you a great deal, Mya. More than perhaps I ought to, even. But I don't want to rush into this." He curled his fingers around her jaw, thumb rubbing along the bone with a gentle motion, and carefully turned her head so that she was looking up at him. "I don't want you to be hurt. And, if I am honest, I don't wish to be hurt either. That's why we have to take this slow, you understand? A few days is not enough time. I can't bear the thought of this going wrong and bringing you pain."

It was already bringing her pain. Mya didn't say that. In any other situation, Kayden would have been right. To rush into something so intense, after only knowing each other for a week, would be foolish. But Mya couldn't shake the way that she felt. She was certain that they'd known each other before, somewhere. Somehow. And if that was true, then she wasn't rushing. And it wasn't foolish.

"This isn't going to go wrong," Mya said, forcing the words to come out more certain than she felt them.

"You can't be sure of that." Kayden's tone was careful, but the words still ached.

"I just... I just am." Mya looked up into those dark eyes that were so strangely familiar. "I know that you don't believe me, but I'm sure that we knew each other before. That we were happy, before. And we can be that way again, Kayden. I know it."

Kayden sighed, and shifted, untangling himself from her and sitting up.

"Say it's true," he said. "That we knew each other somewhere, before we both lost our memories. That does not mean that something won't go wrong now." He looked down at her and sighed. "You don't know how the relationship ended, for one. And even if it was perfect up until the moment that I forgot you existed, we are different people now than we were then, with entirely different lives. There's nothing to say that the relationship that worked before will work again."

Cold without Kayden's warmth wrapped around her, Mya reached down and caught the edge of the blanket, pulling it up to her shoulders. "I just know," she said. "That I can't imagine a life without you in it."

His expression softened. Reaching out, he took her hand in his own. "Mya," he said slowly. "Can you understand my concern, with this?" He looked down at their hands, together against his knee, back up at her. "That you can say that after such a short time... Have you spoken to the doctor at all about the memories you've been having? And the dreams?"

Mya swallowed past a tight ache in her throat. "Yes," she said. "I mentioned them. He said I shouldn't be too concerned, since I'm no longer experiencing other symptoms. He did suggest that maybe I was replacing someone else with you. Feeling emotions for you that belong to someone else, because you are here and they are not. But I don't believe that."

"No?" Kayden met her gaze. "Why is that?"

"Because I would know," Mya said. "I'm sure that I would. And if I was truly in love with someone else, why would I put you in his place, unless I had feelings for you? It just doesn't seem as though it makes sense to me."

"I did save your life," Kayden said. "That could very well be the reason you feel such an attachment to me. I brought you out of that building when you would have died there. It is a more intimate thing than most would guess."

"If it were just that, maybe," Mya said. "But it's more than that. It's the dreams. And the way that... I know what you want before you tell me. I know how to touch you. I know what you like. And you know the same about me. I can tell. If I were putting you in someone else's place in my memories, I would not know your body the way that I do."

His expression shifted, as though he was not quite certain how to respond to that. She saw him start to speak. Stop again. He knew what she referred to, and she could see in the way that he tried and failed to deny it even to himself, that he knew she was right. If they had been strangers, how was their connection so intimate? "For a woman I ought to be calling insane," Kayden said finally. "You are surprisingly convincing."

Mya laughed. "Insane? Is that so?"

"Utterly mad," Kayden answered, and Mya drew him down toward her, leaning up to pull him into a kiss.

"Only because you make me so," she said as their lips met.

They sank down together to the mattress, and for a time, Mya forgot entirely about her worries, and her memories, and knew only Kayden. In the quiet that followed, curled together, they slept, and for once she did not dream.

Chapter 21

Beyond the relative sanctuary of the convent, the war that had swallowed Europe whole went on. Food, which had not been in particularly plentiful supply to begin with, grew more scarce. On the nights she and Kayden ventured to the mess hall, Mya heard whispers of battles in Russia, and the Allies moving in. From occupied Paris and the towns around came more reports of arrests. But in the convent, all was for the most part quiet. The calm before the storm, Kayden said, when she voiced the observation. As the days passed, Mya became convinced he was right. Their little corner of the world could not avoid the war forever.

She wasn't certain if it was that knowledge, or something else, that seemed to hang over her head in the two weeks that followed Kayden's admission that he was afraid to move too quickly on whatever was between them. Though Kayden stayed mostly in the convent, spending his nights with her, and though each day she could see him forgetting his reasons to deny what they shared, she could not help the tightness in her chest. The way she felt as though something was about to go terribly wrong.

She woke early in the morning to Kayden rustling around pulling clothes on. Still groggy with sleep, Mya blinked her eyes open and watched him from the bed, following his progress across the room. He looked like he was in a hurry.

"Are you going out?" she asked.

"Unfortunately," Kayden said. "I didn't mean to wake you."

"When will you return?"

He shook his head. "I can't say. It'll depend on the state of things out there, I think. There's a chance it could just be a false alarm, but if I'm not returned by tonight, don't panic. I may stay with my regiment if things run late."

Mya slid from under the sheets and paced across the room, wrapping herself around Kayden from behind. "I'll miss you," she said softly.

"And I you," Kayden answered, turning to wrap his arms around her and draw her in close. "But I'll be content in the knowledge that you are here, safe, and waiting for my return."

She tried to find a smile for him. It was a little uncertain, but he seemed to accept it, because he smiled back at her, and leaned down to steal a brief kiss before he snatched up his jacket and hurried out the door.

Mya, left standing alone in the room, watched him go, and silently prayed for his safe return.

With Kayden gone, there was not much to do in the room. She glanced at the bed, but his departure had chased any remaining chance of sleep away, and so she pulled the blankets back into place, smoothing them out and laying the pillows on top, before she moved to her little chest to dress for the day.

"He'll return safely," she said aloud, hoping that hearing the words spoken would make the nervous tension knotting in her stomach loosen. "It's nothing serious."

It could be something serious. Mya tried to ignore that thought as she buttoned up her shirt and pulled on her trousers, bending to lace up her boots. If it was something serious, it would be handled, and Kayden would return. She just had to hold to that knowledge. They had not been brought together just to be torn apart again, surely.

When she was clothed, her hair combed back and braided, Mya left the room behind and headed out into the hall, making her way to the doctor's office. He was there, bent over some files at his desk, wearing a consternated frown.

"Doctor," Mya said. He had tried more than once over recent days to get her to use his name, but Mya always felt a little strange at the thought. "Good morning."

"Ah." He looked up. "Good morning, Mya. I trust you slept well?"

"I did," Mya said. "Thank you."

"And how are you feeling?" He stood up, leaving the files he'd been looking at behind, and came to stand in front of her. "Any trouble with your head? Any success in retrieving your memories?"

He asked the questions like he already knew the answers, which Mya supposed that he did. Her head had not hurt for some time, and asking about it was really just his way of making certain that she didn't have any other physical complaints, Mya was sure. As for her memories, she did not think those were coming back, and she could tell by his tone that he didn't either. If they had been gone for this long, there was little chance that she would make a miraculous recovery.

Mya shook her head. "No. It's the same as always."

"As I thought." He frowned, and turned away, looking for something. Likely her file. Thanks to her efforts in organization, he found it rather quickly, and flicked through it, nodding along to whatever he was reading. "In that case," he went on, finally, setting the file aside. "I think you are quite healed from your injury. Or as healed as you are going to be, unfortunately. And I think, Mya, that you might consider leaving this place."

She stared at him. "Leaving?"

It was obvious that he'd expected her objection. He simply nodded. "This is a military hospital in occupied territory. While it may have been safe thus far, the war grows worse, and it is moving closer. The Germans have increased their sweeps of the countryside, and they are increasingly being seen in the area. Whatever happens here in the next weeks or months, it will be messy, and you are in no way obligated to be part of it."

"But—" Mya paused, trying to gather words. "My life is here," she said. "I have work in the hospital. Or work enough to keep me busy, and I get food and board in return for it. That's all that I need. Everyone that I know is here." *Kayden is here.* "I couldn't simply leave."

"They will likely ask civilians to evacuate if the battle lines come this way," the doctor said. "I'm not telling you that you must go now, or that we will throw you out, I am merely suggesting a course of action which might be in your best interest."

"I appreciate the thought, Doctor. But truly, I'm happy here." Mya met his eyes. "There is nowhere I would rather be."

"Suit yourself, then," he said, resigned, and turned back to his desk.

Mya went about her duties, running things back and forth, and seeing what aid she could provide, but the words wouldn't leave her thoughts. She hadn't considered leaving, or where she might go after this place. Her thoughts of the future had all been too bound up in Kayden. Some part of her, she realized, had expected to follow him, wherever he went. But would she be able to do that? He was military, and they were not married. Even if they had been, were he ordered to the front she would hardly be allowed to tag on along.

Where did that leave her? Should she go, as the doctor had suggested? Search for somewhere that she would be safe from the ravages of war? Or should she remain here as long as he could, attempting to convince Kayden that they were meant to be together?

They were questions she didn't have answers for.

Kayden did not return when night fell, and Mya curled up in the bed alone, feeling it stretching out on either side of her in empty expanse. She missed the warmth of his body against her own, and the strength of his arms around her. She missed the sound of his breathing, soft and steady. Worry grew steadily stronger.

He would be well, she reminded herself. It was only a little trip, and he would return. He was likely back already, sleeping safely with his regiment. As she should be sleeping. Mya closed her eyes, and tried to force herself to drift off, but she had no such luck. Overhead, she heard the drone of planes. There were no bombs dropped. Perhaps they fell elsewhere. She couldn't have said.

As the night turned on toward morning, she grew drowsy, and though she was not yet asleep, she was drifting somewhere between there and awake when she heard the door open, heard footsteps crossing the room. There was a quiet thwump of fabric falling in a heap, and then Kayden was crawling into the tiny cot-bed beside her, pulling her against his chest. Mya breathed out a sigh of relief and curled into his arms, grateful for the new warmth. The closeness. His hand slid through her hair, and sleep beckoned, pulling her down.

She woke unsure if she had actually felt Kayden, or if the whole thing had been some kind of dream. But he was there, beside her in the bed, solid and real. He had come in the night before after all. As she looked down at him, he shifted, and then woke, eyes opening.

"Good morning," Mya said.

"And to you," Kayden answered, reaching up to tuck a lock of wayward hair behind her ear. The motion became a caress. "Did you sleep well?"

"Better, once you got back," she admitted. "I was worried."

"You needn't have been," he said gently. "It was a simple mission. No one was wounded."

"But there was fighting?"

"There's always fighting." Kayden pulled her back down so that she lay with her head on his chest. "But it was very brief, and we won." She could hear the smile in his voice. "I don't think they were expecting us, actually."

"I'm just glad you're back," Mya said. She took a breath and let it go, wondering if she ought to mention what she had been told. "The doctor suggested that I leave."

"Leave?" Kayden sounded startled.

"Somewhere safer," Mya said. "He believes that the war is getting closer, and that I'll be in danger."

There was a moment's pause. Mya listened to the sound of Kayden's heart beating under her ear. It had picked up pace with her words. She wondered what was going through his mind.

"He's right that you would be safer elsewhere," Kayden said at last. "The fighting is moving in nearer, and if you remain there's a chance you'll be caught up in it." He paused again, like he wasn't sure whether he should add the rest.

Mya waited.

Someone went by in the hall, boots thumping against the floor. Kayden sighed.

"You might want to consider his suggestion."

Chapter 22

"You look as though you are deep in thought."

Mya lifted her gaze from the tray of medical instruments she was absentmindedly arranging and found one of the nuns gazing back at her with steady brown eyes, waiting for answer.

"Just considering options," she said.

The other woman nodded, stepping around Mya to set something on one of the other trays. "If you want to discuss them, I'm always willing to listen."

Mya sighed. She wasn't sure whether she wanted to talk about them or not, to be honest, but the sister's expression was kind, and on the few occasions they had spoken in the midst of their work for the hospital, Mya had appreciated the comments she had to make. She decided that it couldn't hurt to actually speak to someone else before she decided.

"The doctor told me yesterday that I should leave here for somewhere safer, before the fighting comes any nearer. And someone I trust has backed him up."

And that was the problem, wasn't it? Because no matter how well things had been going, Mya couldn't help but wonder if it was a simple way for Kayden to split from her. Though he had never accepted the idea of soul mates, she thought she had seen a change in him, had felt as though he was coming around to her way of thinking. But it had only been two weeks, and maybe she had misinterpreted things. Or maybe there had been a change, and it had concerned him, and this was his way of ending things before they moved to a place he wasn't comfortable or happy with.

"You're deciding whether to stay or go, then, no?" The sister—Mya thought her name might be Constance—asked. She said the words as though she already knew the answer, and was simply trying to get Mya to talk again.

"Yes," Mya said. "And there's a part of me that wants to stay here. I feel at home in the convent, and I'm doing something useful. If I leave, there's no guarantee I'll find something as fulfilling to do with my life." She turned to the sink to scrub out one of the bowls that had been used for feeding a man in her rotation of care. "But if I stay here, maybe I'm missing something better that's waiting out there. Or maybe I'm making a nuisance of myself and I'm just not aware of it."

Sister Constance laughed. "Believe me, Miss Boyle, you're not making a nuisance of yourself. Your work here is very appreciated. Should you choose to remain, I'm certain it would go on being so. But if I may, I have one piece of advice to offer."

"I would be glad to hear it." Mya turned off the water, and turned back around to look at Sister Constance, waiting.

"Do not let your fears drive you," she said. "Don't only stay because you worry that you'll not find fulfillment beyond our walls. But don't leave only to run from something. It's better to deal with your problems today than to leave them until tomorrow, no matter how tempting it might be."

It was good advice.

As the day went on, Mya turned it over in her mind, trying to decide what conclusion it led to. If she left, was she running from her problems? Or would it simply be the prudent thing to do? Staying with Kayden was what she wanted, but Kayden was a soldier. That he had remained in the city so long during war was a minor miracle; to expect him to continue to stay where she could be with him was wishful thinking and nothing more. If she remained just because she knew the convent and the people in it, and never explored the wider world, would she be satisfied?

In the end, she came to a decision.

If Kayden didn't want her, she would leave. They had been right about it being dangerous. And she should return to Scotland, search for her family. If Kayden didn't want her, maybe they would.

She finished work in the afternoon, and made her way back toward the room where she was staying, still wondering if she had made the right choice. Maybe she ought to talk to Kayden. It could hardly hurt anything. Up ahead, she heard voices, both of them familiar, and paused.

"Do you think she'll go, then?" That one belonged to Captain Taylor.

Mya pressed herself back against the wall, heart beating faster. Was this proof that Kayden did want her to leave after all?

"I think she can be talked around to it," Kayden's deeper voice answered. "She's a clever lass, and this is no place for her, in truth."

They *were* talking about her. Mya bit her lip, trying not to let her breathing make any sort of sound. He did want her to leave. Wanted to make sure that she was talked around to going. Heart clenching, Mya started to turn away.

"And what about your feelings?"

The question stopped her in her tracks. She paused, waiting to hear Kayden's answer. This was the thing that would tell her for certain whether she ought to stay with him or go.

"I will miss her," Kayden said, softer than he had spoken before. Mya had to strain to hear. "I have resisted it, but there is this... connection between us. I cannot deny that it exists." He sighed. "She's the best thing in my life, Taylor. What will I do when she's gone?"

Captain Taylor's answer was a low murmur that Mya couldn't pick the words out of, and she gave up on her eavesdropping as the sound of boots coming down the hall alerted her to someone around the corner behind her. She hurried back toward her room, ducking her head a little as she moved past the hall where

Kayden and Captain Taylor must have been standing, though she doubted it would do anything to stop them recognizing her. But there was no call of greeting, and when she looked up, both of them were already gone.

Kayden would miss her. The knowledge thrummed under her skin, warm and effervescent. He saw their connection, at last. That was enough.

It was more than enough.

Chapter 23

"I want to stay," Mya said almost before Kayden had finished walking in the door.

He stared at her. "What?"

"I said," Mya repeated. "I want to stay. Here. With you."

His eyebrows drew together as he pulled the door carefully shut at his back and walked across the room to sit on the edge of the bed she never slept in. "Mya, you know that I... I would love you to stay. But it isn't safe, and it's only going to be getting worse. I have to ship out when my regiment does. I won't always be here with you. Or to protect you."

"I don't care." Mya got up from the edge of the bed and sank into his lap instead, wrapping herself around him. "I want to remain here. The danger doesn't frighten me. Here I am doing something useful, too. I know that I'm not the most important volunteer at the hospital, but what I do matters."

For an instant, Kayden was still beneath her, and then he wrapped his arms around her and held her close, and Mya laid her head against his shoulder. "I would never say that what you do isn't important. But I think you can do it somewhere else. Somewhere that you're less likely to be harmed." His embrace tightened. "I can't bear the thought of you hurt, Mya."

Mya lifted her head, and found his mouth with hers, her arms sliding around his neck. The kiss was hard and desperate, full of want that neither of them was sure they'd be able to express in the coming days. Mya rocked herself down against him, and felt him growing hard. She moaned softly, the sound swallowed by the kiss.

"Mya," he said when they fell apart for air.

She didn't give him time to finish. Just kissed him again. He was tense for only a moment, and then he was sliding a hand down to curl around her backside and dragging her closer. Mya went more than willingly.

The kisses deepened, and grew hungrier. Hands tangled in hair and slid over bodies. Mya writhed on Kayden's lap. She didn't want to wait any longer. She wanted him. Now.

"Kayden," she said in the brief instant that he allowed her to pull in a breath before he was claiming her mouth again. Despite her desire to speak, she melted into the kiss with a sigh, and it was a long moment before she remembered what she had been going to say.

"Kayden," she said again, breathless. "I need you. Please."

That seemed to be all the prompting that it took, because Kayden's hands were on the fastenings of her clothes an instant later, and he was unbuttoning her trousers and pulling them down her thighs. It took some maneuvering, but he got her out of them, eager fingers working on her shirt buttons. Mya followed suit, stripping him out of his clothes just as urgently as he was stripping her out of hers.

"Kayden," she breathed. "Kayden." The word was the only one she could remember how to say.

In moments, they were both completely bare, and Kayden's hands curled around her hips were lifting her. Mya reached back and curled a hand around the length of him, a groan leaving her throat as she guided him inside, her body sinking down until her thighs met his and she was deliciously full.

"Come on, lass," Kayden growled.

He helped her slide herself up, and then back down again, picking up a rhythm that matched the one her body was moving to. Both of them were panting, moaning. Mya wanted to stay like this forever, wrapped up in Kayden. She curled her fingers around his shoulders and used the grip as leverage to move with the pace that Kayden had set, rolling her hip to make them both spiral upward toward ecstasy.

There was nothing slow or gentle about them together in that moment. It was all passion. All hunger and need. Mya tossed her head, her hair falling over her shoulders, and Kayden leaned down to kiss her hard as she continued to ride him.

"I want—" Stars dazzled across Mya's eyelids and she couldn't recall what she had meant to say. Words slipped through her thoughts like water.

"Fuck," Kayden groaned.

There were no words after that, only the two of them. Mya's nails raked down Kayden's shoulders, and he leaned in and bit down on the curve where neck met shoulder, just hard enough to almost hurt. She gasped.

It wasn't going to be long; neither of them were going to last. Another thrust. Kayden's hand left her hip and slid upward to cup the weight of her breast, thumb rubbing circles over her nipple. His mouth found hers once more.

It was more than Mya could take. She picked up the pace, and one of her hands slipped down between them so she could rub her fingers over her clit. Kayden's rhythm faltered. Her thighs trembled. He rocked up into her, hard, his hands pulling her down, and that was it.

They went over the edge together, sobbing wrecked syllables through panting breaths. Kayden's fingers tightened around her hips, then relaxed. Kayden let himself fall back against the bed, and Mya sank down with him, still trying to remember the proper way to breathe.

"I love you," Kayden said, his arm wrapping around her waist.

Mya froze. Her head lifted, and she looked up at Kayden, who was looking down at her with complete sincerity in his dark eyes. Her breath caught.

"I love you too," she answered.

The words felt exactly as they should have on her tongue.

Chapter 24

Later, when they had both bathed and eaten and were once more in bed, curled around each other under the blankets, Mya told Kayden again that she wanted to stay. His hand stroked circles over her back, and her head rested on his shoulder, the beat of his heart steady under her ear.

"I don't think you should," he said. "And before you go getting all up in arms over it, lass, let me explain to you why."

Mya swallowed the words that had been on her tongue and waited for him to speak.

"I'm shipping out."

She startled half upright, staring down at him. "What? When? Why didn't you tell me?"

"I hadn't told you yet because I only just found out myself, while you were in the shower," Kayden said. "It'll be tomorrow."

"*Tomorrow?*"

"Yes. It's a situation that's time sensitive, and they need us out as soon as we can embark. They wanted us to leave tonight, but there were supplies to be gathered."

Mya's shoulders slumped. "But you only just... I don't want to be separated from you."

"Nor I from you," Kayden answered. "But it is the way of war. And we do what we must." His eyes met hers. "I will come and find you when the fighting is done, lass. I promise. And anything that you need in the meantime, I will take care of it."

"You don't have to do that."

"No," he agreed. "But I love you, and I wish to take care of you. I've money and you do not. So I have no trouble giving you some to help keep you on your feet while I'm away." He smiled. "So long as you promise to wait for me."

"I'll wait forever, if that's what it takes," Mya answered passionately. "I'm not losing you again, Kayden."

He drew her down to him again, and Mya let herself go, wrapping an arm close around his chest. She hadn't said it, but she was afraid. He was sending her out of danger, while walking into it himself. What if something happened to him?

"What is it, lass?" Kayden asked, hand stilling on her back.

"I'm worried," Mya answered, throat tight. "That's not a strong enough word for it. To be honest, I'm afraid. I'm so afraid that something will happen to you, and I'll be left somewhere, waiting for a lover who will never come home. What if I can't handle it?"

Kayden wrapped her closer in his arms, and Mya closed her eyes, breathing in the scent of him and feeling safe against the bulk of his chest.

"You can," he said, voice soft, but sure. "You were given this life because you are strong enough to live it."

Mya took a deep breath and let it out again. She was strong enough to live it. And Kayden would come home to her. She simply had to trust in that.

"Mya," Kayden said.

She lifted her head to look up at him, and found herself suddenly in motion. He had sat up, pulling her with him, and was looking at her with something she couldn't quite read in his expression. He looked into her eyes. His chin dipped in a nod, as though he was confirming something to himself.

"I know," he said. "That this is somewhat unorthodox." A smile flashed across his face. "And that I should likely be putting on some pants before I do it, but I don't think I'm much in the mood to wait."

Mya stared at him. Her pulse picked up. Surely it couldn't be what she thought it was. He couldn't be-

His hands closed gently over hers. "Mya Boyle," he said. "I know that I'm a soldier running off to battle, and that this is absolutely insane, but I want to know if you'd do me the honor of being my wife when all this is done?"

For a moment, she was too shocked to say anything at all. She saw trepidation twist his smile, the instant where he thought that maybe she wasn't going to reply. That he had made a mistake. Laughter bubbled up in her chest. "Yes!" she said, laughing and crying at the same time. "Absolutely yes, Kayden McGregor. I don't care if it's crazy. I'll marry you." She wrapped herself around him, speaking between kisses. "I'd marry you right this minute if we could find someone to do it."

His chuckle was warm, and fond. "I think the chaplain is asleep at this hour, lass. But I promise you, when this war is done, we'll have a wedding. The kind of wedding you deserve."

Mya didn't care if the wedding was the two of them and a chaplain running through the ceremony while bombs fell outside, so long as Kayden was beside her, but she supposed waiting a little longer than a month for the actual marriage was the better choice. At least he had asked.

Now, whatever happened, she was his.

That night, as she slept, she dreamed that she ran. Strong and graceful. Her heart beat steady behind her ribs, and her legs carried her easily over the earth, feet hardly seeming to touch the ground. The wind streamed over her, filling her lungs with fresh, sweet air.

Then her footing changed, and she stumbled.

Overhead, thunder crashed, unrolling itself across the clouds with a deep, displeased rumble. Lighting forked down, burning the skeletons of trees across the backs of her eyelids in silhouette.

Rain was falling, sharp as needles. It pricked against her skin and chilled her through. To her left, she could hear the sound of surf falling against shoreline, violent and ragged as the wind that drove it. She shivered, and pushed her stumbling legs forward.

Ahead, she could see a vague white form through the darkness of the storm. Always out of reach. She pushed herself faster. Trying. Straining.

Thunder boomed, and the ground went out from under her. She fell.

There was nothing for her grasping hands to catch. Only emptiness beneath her, and pain. Pain that ripped through her chest and left her gasping in shock, struggling to breathe. She cried out, but no sound left her lips.

And then she woke.

The other side of the bed was empty. Mya looked at it for a long moment, not comprehending. There was a note on the pillow. Hand trembling, she reached out and picked it up.

My darling lass,

We had to be off earlier than expected. You slept so deeply I didn't want to wake you. Watch for my letters.

I will find you. Always.

All my love,

Kayden.

Epilogue

She wasn't sure how it had even been delivered, how he had got it to her. There was, as far as she knew, no reliable post. Letters came for the doctor on occasion, and far less frequently for some of the patients, usually the ones who had been there the longest, but she had received nothing. Nobody knew she was there. Until now. When, of course, she was not staying. Soon she would be gone across the channel to Scotland, where Kayden had a house waiting. She was glad she had been there to receive the package at all.

Perhaps he had asked army friends to courier it to her. Mya wasn't sure. She didn't really care how it had come, to be honest. It was the fact of it that mattered. It had been waiting for her when she had walked down to the room that she had beaten into some semblance of efficiency for the doctor. The folders were stored in boxes, in alphabetical order, the paperwork likewise sorted. It had taken her just minutes to sort the papers of the previous night into their places, and then, standing back, she had felt, for a weird, disorientating moment, a sense of finality, as though her job there was done. Finished. Completed.

Then she had looked down into the shallow cardboard box that now served as an in-box for the doctor, and she had seen the small, innocuous parcel addressed to her. She had placed it into one of the many pockets in her army trousers, and then, for a while, her day had become busy with new casualties being brought in, and she had put it from her mind. In fact, it was not until she was walking back to her room and she put her hand into her pocket, and her fingers brushed the little package, that she had been fully reminded of it.

Mya hadn't taken it from her pocket then, but she'd wrapped her fingers around it, and held it close within her hand until she was safe within her room, and it was only once she was there, in the place that had become a little sanctuary for her and Kayden, sitting on the bed that they had so often shared, that she had brought it out and looked at it. She was torn, half of her wanted to rip it open and see, immediately, what it contained, but something held her back, some half-formed worry, a hesitation she could not have explained, had she been asked.

She peeled it open slowly, one layer of wrapping at a time, until she uncovered a small box, with her name scribed into the lid, and for a moment she stared at the three letters as though trying to make sense of them, then, all hesitation forgotten, she opened it and took out the ring within. It was beautiful, the stone was not a particularly large one, but it was beautifully set within a little raised square, the metal that housed it fine and ornate, with decorative swallow tail shoulders joining it to a plain gold band. She loved it the moment she saw it, and her only regret, as she sat on the bed, looking at it, was that Kayden wasn't there to place it around her finger.

She looked at it for a long time, admiring it, turning it this way and that and watching the way the light glinted from the stone, and then finally she slipped her finger into it. It fit perfectly, as she had known that it would, and the cold metal warmed quickly. Still she looked at it, though now it was her finger, her hand, that she twisted, looking at it against her skin.

"Kayden." She whispered his name softly, as though she could conjure him, as though speaking the word would make him appear. But of course he did not. She sighed and looked the wrapping over carefully. There was no return address anywhere on it, and yet, she decided, she would go and fetch paper and pen to the room later. She would write and tell him that she had received it, that she loved it. That she loved him. She would figure out how to get it to him, there would be a way. After all, she thought, if, in the chaos of this terrible war, they had managed to find one another, and to find love together, then getting a letter to him should not prove to be so very hard.

Mya lay back on the bed, smiling as the light glittered against the diamond when she moved her hand, though she determined, right there and then, that she would not be one of those newly engaged women who came at everyone ring first. That made her stifle a laugh, her hand coming up to cover her mouth, but as she lifted it she suddenly felt a pain that was almost familiar, and at first she thought it was her shoulder, and she let her hand drop again, but the pain grew, moved until it was undeniably in her chest, in her heart. Still, through it all there was a sense of familiarity of having been here before. At the same time, her heart felt as though it was ripped from her, and she was filled with dread, not for herself, or for her own pain, but for Kayden.

She didn't know how long it lasted, perhaps moments, perhaps hours, perhaps an eternity, but when she came back she was saying his name, over and over again, and her face was wet with tears. Where her heart had been there was only ice, or emptiness.

"Kayden." She pushed herself upright, looking down at the ring on her hand, but it offered no comfort, it only glittered cold as ice, cold as her heart. Somehow she got herself from the bed, and suddenly, feeling claustrophobic and confined, she went over to the window, moved the curtain just a crack so that she could see out but no light could escape. "Kayden."

How could everything suddenly feel so different now? So hopeless? How could she suddenly feel so alone? Stranded in this place she did not belong. Outside she heard planes, and she wondered if they ever stopped. It was somehow fitting, she thought, that they could come to bring destruction, when she felt so destroyed. She looked up, but the city was dark, and the sky was as black, as devoid of light as the ground. Through the fog, she thought she saw a flash of white, a horned head, but that might only have been her imagination. She let the curtain fall.

And then she heard them. The shells, and the familiar sound of them falling. They were close, she realized, closer than she had ever known, perhaps even closer than the shell outside had been. And then there was a thud, and it grew louder, became a dull boom that was above her and below her at the same time, and then suddenly there was darkness, and nothing.

Nothing at all.

THE END
NEXT: A Royal Bride

A Royal Bride: Moment in Time #4

"You were given this life because you're strong enough to live it."

Mya Boyle finds herself once again in the highlands of Scotland. In a time she doesn't remember, injured, with no title, no lands, no memory of the life she's lived.

A handsome, richly dressed hero comes to her rescue. Her Highlander... and a prince. She's sure she knows him, feels the memory of him will come back at any moment. However, Prince Kayden McGregor swears he doesn't know her, that they've only met that day for the first time.

Love between them is inevitable.

Threatened by country as a traitor, Mya must prove that she is not after the crown. The more she digs into her past and remembers, the more Kayden seems to forget.

When the hands of man threaten to tear them apart, will Fate intervene?

Or has time run out for Mya and Kayden? Can she show him that their love is eternal, before it's too late?

"Time changes everyone."

A Moment in Time Series

More by Lexy Timms:

**Sometimes the heart needs a different kind of saving...
find out if Charity Thompson will find a way of saving forever
in this hospital setting Best-Selling Romance by Lexy Timms**

Charity Thompson wants to save the world, one hospital at a time. Instead of finishing med school to become a doctor, she chooses a different path and raises money for hospitals – new wings, equipment, whatever they need. Except there is one hospital she would be happy to never set foot in again—her fathers. So of course he hires her to create a gala for his sixty-fifth birthday. Charity can't say no. Now she is working in the one place she doesn't want to be. Except she's attracted to Dr. Elijah Bennet, the handsome playboy chief.

Will she ever prove to her father that's she's more than a med school dropout? Or will her attraction to Elijah keep her from repairing the one thing she desperately wants to fix?

** This is NOT Erotica. It's Romance and a love story. **

* This is Part 1 of an Eight book Romance Series. It does end on a cliff-hanger*

Managing the Bosses Series
The Boss
Book 1 IS FREE!

Jamie Connors has given up on finding a man. Despite being smart, pretty, and just slightly overweight, she's a magnet for the kind of guys that don't stay around.

Her sister's wedding is at the foreground of the family's attention. Jamie would be find with it if her sister wasn't pressuring her to lose weight so she'll fit in the maid of honor dress, her mother would get off her case and her ex-boyfriend wasn't about to become her brother-in-law.

Determined to step out on her own, she accepts a PA position from billionaire Alex Reid. The job includes an apartment on his property and gets her out of living in her parent's basement.

Jamie has to balance her life and somehow figure out how to manage her billionaire boss, without falling in love with him.

Hades' Spawn MC Series
One You Can't Forget
Book 1 is FREE
Emily Rose Dougherty is a good Catholic girl from mythical Walkerville, CT. She had somehow managed to get herself into a heap trouble with the law, all because an ex-boyfriend has decided to make things difficult.
Luke "Spade" Wade owns a Motorcycle repair shop and is the Road Captain for Hades' Spawn MC. He's shocked when he reads in the paper that his old high school flame has been arrested. She's always been the one he couldn't forget.
Will destiny let them find each other again? Or what happens in the past, best left for the history books?

The Recruiting Trip

Aspiring college athlete Aileen Nessa is finding the recruiting process beyond daunting. Being ranked #10 in the world for the 100m hurdles at the age of eighteen is not a fluke, even though she believes that one race, where everything clinked magically together, might be. American universities don't seem to think so. Letters are pouring in from all over the country.

As she faces the challenge of differentiating between a college's genuine commitment to her or just empty promises from talent-seeking coaches, Aileen heads to the University of Gatica, a Division One school, on a recruiting trip. Her best friend dares who to go just to see the cute guys on the school's brochure.

The university's athletic program boasts one of the top hurdlers in the country. Tyler Jensen is the school's NCAA champion in the hurdles and Jim Thorpe recipient for top defensive back in football. His incredible blue-green eyes, confident smile and rock hard six pack abs mess with Aileen's concentration.

His offer to take her under his wing, should she choose to come to Gatica, is a temping proposition that has her wondering if she might be with an angel or making a deal with the devil himself.

Seeking Justice
Book 1 – is FREE

Rachel Evans has the life most people could only dream of: the promise of an amazing job, good looks, and a life of luxury. The problem is, she hates it. She tries desperately to avoid getting sucked into the family business and hides her wealth and name from her friends. She's seen her brother trapped in that life, and doesn't want it. When her father dies in a plane crash, she reluctantly steps in to become the vice president of her family's company, Syco Pharmaceuticals.

Detective Adrien Deluca and his partner have been called in to look at the crash. While Adrien immediately suspects not everything about the case is what it seems, he has trouble convincing his partner. However, soon into the investigation, they uncover a web of deceit which proves the crash was no accident, and evidence points toward a shadowy group of people. Now the detective needs find the proof.

To what lengths will Deluca go to get it?

Fortune Riders MC Series
NOW AVAILABLE!

Undercover Series - Book 1, PERFECT FOR ME, is FREE!

The city of Pittsburgh keeps its streets safe, partly thanks to Lt. Grady Rivers. The police officer is fiercely intelligent who specializes in undercover operations. It is this set of skills that are sought by New York's finest. Grady is thrown from his hometown onto the New York City underworld in order to stop one of the largest drug rings in the northeast. The NYPD task him with uncovering the identity of the organization's mysterious leader, Dean. It will take all of his cunning to stop this deadly drug lord.

Danger lurks around every corner and comes in many shapes. While undercover, he meets a beauty named Lara. An equally intelligent woman and twice as fearless, she works for a local drug dealer who has ties to the organization. Their sorted pasts have these two become close, and soon they develop feelings for one another. But this is not a "Romeo and Juliet" love story, as the star-crossed lovers fight to survive the deadly streets. Grady treads the thin line between the love he feels for her, and his duties as an officer.

Will he get in too deep?

Heart of the Battle Series
Celtic Viking
Book 1 is FREE!
In a world plagued with darkness, she would be his salvation.
No one gave Erik a choice as to whether he would fight or not. Duty to the crown belonged to him, his father's legacy remaining beyond the grave.
Taken by the beauty of the countryside surrounding her, Linzi would do anything to protect her father's land. Britain is under attack and Scotland is next. At a time she should be focused on suitors, the men of her country have gone to war and she's left to stand alone.
Love will become available, but will passion at the touch of the enemy unravel her strong hold first?
Fall in love with this Historical Celtic Viking Romance.

Knox Township, August 1863.

Little Love Affair, Book 1 in the Southern Romance series, by bestselling author Lexy Timms

Sentiments are running high following the battle of Gettysburg, and although the draft has not yet come to Knox, "Bloody Knox" will claim lives the next year as citizens attempt to avoid the Union draft. Clara's brother Solomon is missing, and Clara has been left to manage the family's farm, caring for her mother and her younger sister, Cecelia.

Meanwhile, wounded at the battle of Monterey Pass but still able to escape Union forces, Jasper and his friend Horace are lost and starving. Jasper wants to find his way back to the Confederacy, but feels honor-bound to bring Horace back to his family, though the man seems reluctant.

Now Available:

Coming Soon:

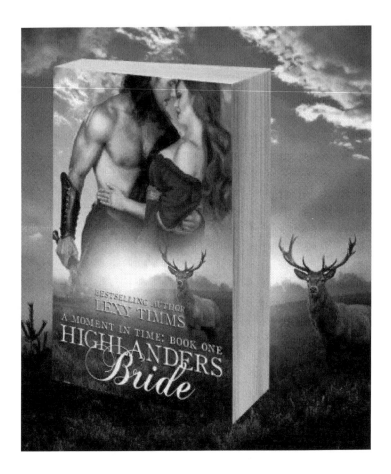

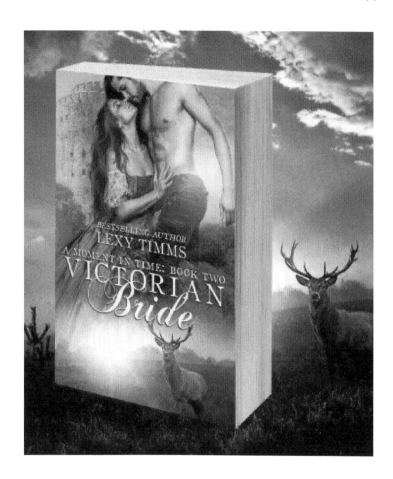

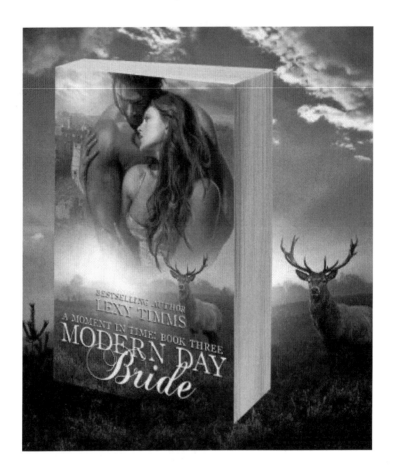

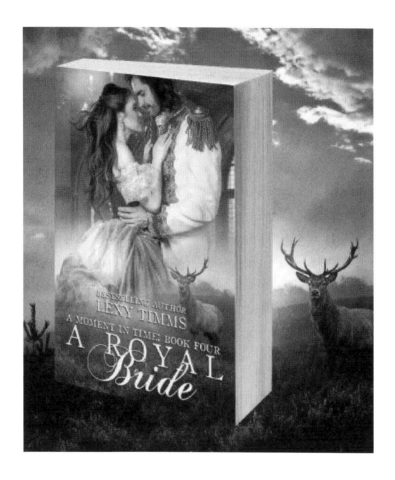

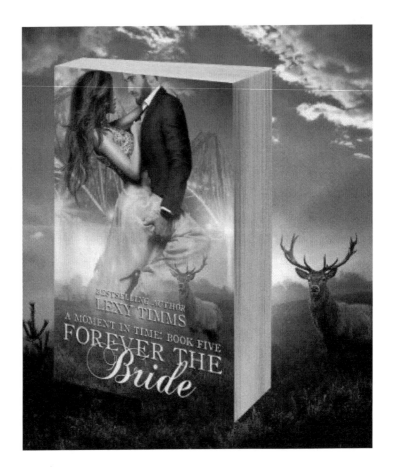

Don't miss out!

Click the button below and you can sign up to receive emails whenever Lexy Timms publishes a new book. There's no charge and no obligation.

Did you love *Modern Day Bride*? Then you should read *Unknown* by Lexy Timms!

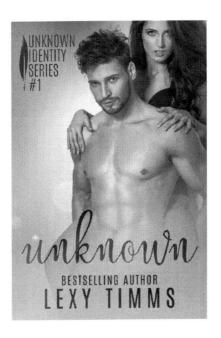

Bestselling romance author, Lexy Timms, brings you a new billionaire contemporary romance series that'll steal your heart and take your breath away.

Unknown - book 1 of the Unknown Identity Series

Life has changed radically for Leslie. Her husband has finally succumbed to his terminal cancer and it's time for her to have a change of scenery. Moving across the country and setting up shop, Leslie takes the months to rebuild her life and figure out what she wants in the future.

Pouring herself into her successful mystery books series she's written, she is a reclusive global sensation writing under a penname.

Leslie realizes that her life is missing the romance she so desperately craved and now she's on the hunt to live her life beyond her grief.

Sooner than she realizes, cupid comes calling in the form of a handsome actor who has no clue she's a successful author. However, he comes with his own personal set of baggage.

Is new love possible after you've laid true love to rest?

Unknown Identity Series

Book 1 - Unknown

Book 2 - Unpublished

Book 3 - Unexposed

Also by Lexy Timms

Alpha Bad Boy Motorcycle Club Triology
Alpha Biker

Conquering Warrior Series
Ruthless

Diamond in the Rough Anthology
Billionaire Rock
Billionaire Rock - part 2

Dominating PA Series
Her Personal Assistant - Part 1
Her Personal Assistant - Part 2
Her Personal Assistant - Part 3
Her Personal Assistant Box Set

Firehouse Romance Series
Caught in Flames
Burning With Desire
Craving the Heat
Firehouse Romance Complete Collection

Fortune Riders MC Series
Billionaire Biker
Billionaire Ransom
Billionaire Misery

Hades' Spawn Motorcycle Club
One You Can't Forget
One That Got Away

One That Came Back
One You Never Leave
Hades' Spawn MC Complete Series

Heart of the Battle Series
Celtic Viking
Celtic Rune
Celtic Mann
Heart of the Battle Series Box Set

Justice Series
Seeking Justice
Finding Justice
Chasing Justice
Pursuing Justice
Justice - Complete Series

Love You Series
Love Life: Billionaire Dance School Hot Romance
Need Love
My Love

Managing the Bosses Series
The Boss
The Boss Too
Who's the Boss Now
Love the Boss
I Do the Boss
Wife to the Boss
Employed by the Boss
Brother to the Boss
Senior Advisor to the Boss
Forever the Boss
Gift for the Boss - Novella 3.5

Whisky Melody
Whisky Harmony

The Debt
The Debt: Part 1 - Damn Horse
The Debt: Complete Collection

The University of Gatica Series
The Recruiting Trip
Faster
Higher
Stronger
Dominate
No Rush

Undercover Series
Perfect For Me
Perfect For You
Perfect For Us

Unknown Identity Series
Unknown
Unexposed
Unpublished

Standalone
Wash
Loving Charity
Summer Lovin'
Christmas Magic: A Romance Anthology
Love & College
Billionaire Heart
First Love
Frisky and Fun Romance Box Collection

Managing the Bosses Box Set #1-3

Made in the USA
Middletown, DE
14 December 2018